Becket's shrine in Canterbury Cathedral. Slowly Lowell lowers his defenses, and as the trip progresses, so does their relationship.

By the time they arrive home, Lowell and Jane have shared the painful secrets that seem to have claimed each of their lives. And they've learned something about themselves. Like Catherine Parr, King Henry's sixth wife, they too are Survivors.

ABOUT THE AUTHOR

Barbara Williams is the author of more than forty books for young readers. A long-time resident of Salt Lake City, Utah, Mrs. Williams is the mother of four grown children and has seven grandchildren. *Beheaded, Survived* is the winner of the Utah Arts Council's 1986 Publication Prize.

BEHEADED, SURVIVED

Beheaded,
Survived

BY BARBARA WILLIAMS

Franklin Watts   New York   London   Toronto   Sydney   1987

Library of Congress Cataloging-in-Publication Data

Williams, Barbara.
    Beheaded, survived.

    Summary: Jane doesn't want any of the other kids on
the tour of England to know she's diabetic, especially
not her new friend, Lowell, who is concealing his own
painful secrets about his family life.
    [1. Diabetes—Fiction. 2. Family problems—
Fiction. 3. England—Fiction] I. Title.
PZ7.W65587Be 1987   [Fic]   87-2035
ISBN 0-531-10403-6 (lib. bdg.)
ISBN 0-531-15071-2

For Elaine, who inspired this story,
For Don and Jan, who encouraged,
And for Matt, Vivian, and especially J.D.,
who lived many of the events with me.

BEHEADED, SURVIVED

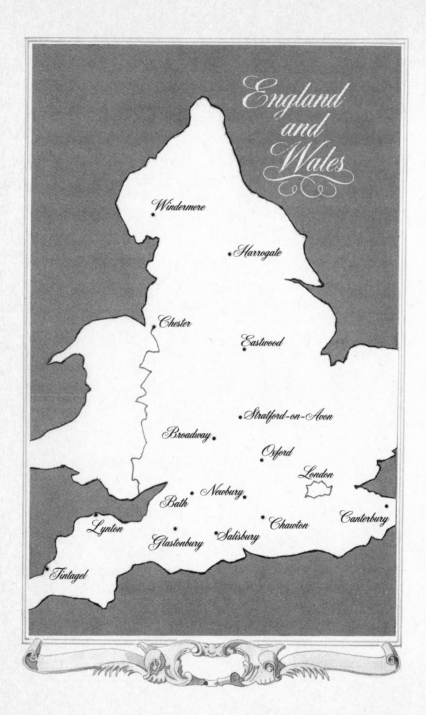

England
and
Wales

Windermere

Harrogate

Chester

Eastwood

Stratford-on-Avon

Broadway

Oxford

London

Newbury

Bath

Chawton

Canterbury

Lynton

Glastonbury Salisbury

Tintagel

"Let's circulate," Courtney suggests.

"Circulate?" I say nervously.

"Circulate," she repeats. A command this time. She starts off, then looks back over her shoulder. "Come on. Don't be dull."

I can't move. My feet are two hunks of mountain.

I shake my head, but Courtney doesn't notice. She is already being un-dull among the other teenagers who have green tapes on the handles of their suitcases. In addition to Courtney and me, there are thirty-eight kids from ten states. I haven't counted or anything. I just know certain essentials (like what to do with the green tape he sent) from the letter signed *Henry J. Phillips, Ph.D., Head-master of Carrington Academy, Sleepy Hollow, Illinois.* Court and I have just flown in from San Francisco to meet him and the others here at the TWA counter at O'Hare Airport at 4:30 p.m.

I see Courtney talking to this blond kid with fly-away hair. He shuffles his feet in some dance step, trying to impress her. Everyone tries to impress my big sister.

Panic sets in as I realize something. We haven't even boarded the plane for London, and already Courtney has abandoned me. Three weeks in England with everyone else circulating and being un-dull and me standing granite-footed with my guide books and Monarch Notes. Why did I choose this trip anyhow? Will it really be better than a month on horseback in Montana, which was Courtney's idea?

Court specializes in vigorous activities like racing horses and breaking hearts. Like Mom and Dad, she's one of the

Beautiful People. I'm the family's token handicapped person. Plain Jane Johnson. Unhealthy and dull.

I'm so dull (Courtney tells me) that when I put on a red dress it turns gray. I'm so dull (Courtney tells me) that I could walk naked into the boys' locker room and no one would see me.

My mother, who was once Miss California, agonizes over what sin she committed against the Almighty to be cursed with a daughter who is imperfect. She asks everyone. Her psychiatrist. Strangers she meets at the health spa. Even God Himself.

I picture her right now in Atherton, California, looking up at the ceiling. "Oh God, what did I ever do to deserve Jane?"

Meanwhile, because she gets tired of worrying about my health, she concentrates on my dullness. She introduces me to the sons of her tennis partners. She buys me books on color coding. She gives me personal tutoring in charm.

Lesson Number One goes like this: When you're at a big gathering and everyone but you seems to be having a good time, you look around the room for someone else who is alone. Then you put a big smile on your face and go over and talk to that person.

Could I really do it? Me?

If I can't, I'll spend a gosh-awful three weeks in Great Britain.

I take a deep breath and look among the green-taped suitcases at the other kids. On paper they're all like me. Between the ages of fourteen and seventeen. Non-troublemakers. Above average academically. (Requirements for Henry Phillips' tours are very explicit.) So why should they frighten me?

I throw back my shoulders to try Lesson One.

Aha! There he is. The other lonely person. Not bad-looking, either. But if he's alone, he must be impaired, too. I study him carefully for his flaw. What is it? Certainly not his hair. Wavy brown. Or his mouth. Sensitive, like

Lord Byron's in that picture on our classroom wall. Maybe he's too thin. Not really. Is his nose too big? Lord Byron (very handsome!) had a strong nose, too.

I picture myself back home telling Brenda all about my summer romance. *"Court had this terrible crush on him, too. But she just wasn't his type. Courtney is so obvious."*

Yes, this kid is a Lord Byron if I ever saw one. I bet he even writes poetry. Definitely the one for me.

I stare at him, sending him we-are-soulmates signals.

He looks at me.

I smile and lift one foot to start in his direction.

He scowls and turns away.

Well, so much for Lesson One.

JANE
*Tuesday, July 30, 5:50 p.m.
Aboard 747*

2

Courtney is sitting next to me, but I'm alone.

"Fantastic," she pants to Fly-Away Hair, as if he were Richard Gere or something. He isn't Richard Gere. He's Scott Tanner from Des Moines, Iowa, whose father owns all those Beef and Bun fast food restaurants. No kidding.

As recently as yesterday Court gave me her critique of Beef and Bun restaurants. "I'd die of starvation before I'd eat there. That name grosses me out. And those commercials are Barf City. An absolute scuz-brain thought them up."

That was yesterday. This is today.

Now she's sitting round-eyed while Scott tells her how his father stumbled across the cute pink-cheeked kid who winks as he delivers the famous television line: "I look for lots of beef on my buns."

Scott's voice doesn't carry above the 747 noises, and I

don't hear much of what he says. Besides, I can tell by the way Court leans toward him that she considers this a private conversation.

For no reason, I start thinking about my new glucometer. If anything happens to it, will I be able to buy one in England small enough to carry in my purse? I check my wallet for the millionth time to make sure I still have the phone number of that doctor in London. But please, God, don't let Henry Phillips hint to the other kids that there's anything different about me. I take a deep breath, refusing to worry anymore.

To the right of me is a lady wearing twelve rings. (I count them again and again.) She doesn't talk to me either. She's reading a paperback called *Starlight* by Debbie Macomber. On the cover is a brunette in a see-through blouse standing on the beach. A man brushes her ear with his lips and fondles her bare shoulder, making her look ready to swoon with ecstasy. She better not. The tide is roaring in.

The woman with the rings smiles, enjoying whatever it is she's reading.

Well, I'll enjoy this trip too! Not every fourteen-year-old is lucky enough to spend three weeks in Britain this summer, visiting all the literary sites her English teacher raves about. Now is a good time to start enjoying the places I'll be seeing by reading about them in advance.

I shuffle through the paperbacks in my green-taped carry-on, wondering which one to read first: Monarch Notes for *The British Romantic Poets*; Monarch Notes for Chaucer's *Canterbury Tales*; Monarch Notes for *British Novelists*; Monarch Notes for T. S. Eliot's *Murder in the Cathedral*; and a real copy of *A Proud Taste for Scarlet and Miniver*. I choose *A Proud Taste for Scarlet and Miniver*, even though it's the only one of the books that I've already read. Five times, as a matter of fact.

I settle back in my seat to find out if Henry II will ever be admitted to heaven. But somehow, after two pages, my mind wanders. New problems of my own keep surfacing. (Will I get through customs without any of the kids on this tour seeing what's in my purse?) Besides, I already learned Henry's outcome five readings ago. With a sigh I close the book and put it back in my carry-on.

Wondering how else to pass the time, I glance across the aisle where the tour director's wife (Sylvia, she told us to call her) is conversing with the kid who scowled at me in the airport. No. Not conversing *with*. Conversing *to*. He barely listens to her but shifts bloodshot eyes around the airplane cabin in a desperate manner, almost as if in pain. Is that it? Is he the token unhealthy person in his family?

Maybe he's stoned.

Mrs. Phillips (I find it hard to call her Sylvia, even in my mind) feels my eyes on them and turns to me with a smile and a wave. So! I'm not going to be ignored by everyone on this trip. Someone has noticed me.

Still, it's the kid I wonder about. Why does he grab his flight bag so angrily? Why does he carry so many notebooks and envelopes? Why does he cover his paper with the other hand while he writes?

LOWELL
Tuesday, July 30, 5:50 p.m.
Aboard 747

3

Die so you can destroy those around you.

Live like the praying mantis. Assume the posture of prayer, and prey, prey, prey on those who love you.

Never love lest you be cannibalized.

Sauce from the barbecued chicken dribbles down Court's chin, and she dabs at it with a paper napkin. "BBQ Chicken Plantation offered with a cup of smoky sauce," she says, parroting the menu the flight attendant gave us. "Who thinks up these scuzzy dinners?"

"Yeah," agrees Scott. "I wish they'd serve pizza on airplanes once in awhile." He bends over his chicken, even though it isn't pizza, and shovels it into his mouth.

I say nothing, having found a new worry. The lady next to me and I seem to be the only people on board who haven't been served. She's too busy with her novel to notice, but I notice enough for both of us. Mother has no doubt arranged for me to receive a special meal, as she did on the other flight out of San Francisco. But this time there are kids around to see that I'm a freak. Kids I'll be spending three weeks with.

Please, Stewardess, whoever you are. Don't yell your lungs out the way that last one did.

Carrying two trays, a flight attendant rushes toward us then, frazzled. Too frazzled to realize that her skirt zipper is undone. Too frazzled to yell her lungs out or even announce softly that she's carrying a special meal.

The stewardess is so frazzled that she doesn't even set the right trays on the right tables. My nose twitches appreciatively as it smells the BBQ Chicken Plantation, and I find myself wondering (as usual) what it would be like to be a real person who eats real food.

Back in Atherton I hear Donald Lieberman, M.D. "I wish all my patients were like you, Jane. I can always count on you to do what I tell you."

Yes. Dependable Jane. Dull, dependable Jane.

Next to me the jeweled fingers set the open novel upside-down on the lap and reach for the carton of skim milk. Skim milk and fish. Doesn't the lady know she has the wrong tray?

Maybe I should let her go ahead and eat my dinner. Maybe I should be un-dependable for a change.

Who me? Of course not. I pick up the tray of barbecued chicken to make the trade. Suddenly I drop it to my table. The kid from across the aisle is studying me with bloodshot eyes.

I turn away, but my hands shake as I feel his eyes still on me, burning, penetrating. Has he guessed my secret? Is he staring to make sure?

My heart pounds.

Jeweled fingers cut the salmon on the table next to mine. I can't let this lady eat my dinner, but I can't stop her, either. Not while that kid is watching. I pretend to cough as I look across the aisle. His eyes are cast down, on his own meal. I look back and see the lady chewing my salmon. Cripes!

Well, eating nothing will be worse than eating this barbecued chicken. I scrape the sauce carefully away and remove the skin from the breast. Mmm. Not bad. Darn good, in fact. I eat more chicken greedily. Then some salad greens. (No salad dressing. No roll and butter.) But some broccoli and corn. More. Soon it's all gone but the Apple Cookie Delight and the Dinner Mint, which I leave untouched.

Already the flight attendants (less frazzled now) are collecting dinner trays because the movie (terribly old, but I don't mind) will start soon. I've seen *Footloose* hundreds of times (in the theater, on our own VCR) but not recently, and anyhow it's fun to watch Kevin Bacon dance. Somehow, though, I feel drowsy and wonder if I can stay awake long enough to justify the money I spent on earphones. Darn that Dramamine Mom insisted I take.

Courtney, who didn't have to take Dramamine, is

burbling to Scott. "Isn't Kevin Bacon absolutely fantastic? You know something? You remind me of him."

Lights go out in the cabin, and the older people—at least the ones who didn't rent headsets—are curling up with pillows and blankets for the night. Some of them have traded seats so they can sit by an empty one and stretch out. I notice that Mrs. Phillips—I mean Sylvia—has vacated the seat across the aisle from me. Her scowling, staring former seatmate removes a flashlight from his flight bag to continue writing. He's weird all right. Why doesn't he turn on his overhead light? He has a stack of envelopes at his elbow. Is he writing letters? How could anyone be homesick already?

LOWELL
Tuesday, July 30, very late
Aboard 747

5

Dear Jill,
    Now that you've abandoned me, there's nothing left in this world. . . .

Dear Chris,
    Whoever told you that women can have anything they want in this world and never pay for it? . . .

Dear Dad,
    My idea is to go home. I have decided to take the next flight back to Phoenix. You won't even be in Scottsdale and won't be bothered by me, so what difference does it make to anyone? . . .

Dear Dr. Cline,
    What makes you think these headaches will stop bothering me? I'd like to tell you about the one right now. It feels like a sledgehammer in my skull. How would you like a sledgehammer in your skull? . . .

JANE
Wednesday, July 31, very early
Aboard 747

6

I'm conscious that it's light outside. Blinds are being raised.

I'm also conscious that I didn't see much of Kevin Bacon last night. I sit up and remove the headset, wondering how long I've been asleep.

"Well, it's about time you woke up," Courtney says. "You kept everyone else on this plane awake with your snoring."

The ring-fingered lady has left the seat next to mine. Did I bother her so much she had to sleep somewhere else?

I don't really have time to feel guilty about that because I have a more immediate concern. I'm ready to explode. Also, Dr. Lieberman has warned me about all the things I must do to adjust my body to the new time zone. The aisles are crowded with people who have similar problems, and I realize I have a long wait. I reach down below the seat in front of me and get my flight bag.

"Boy, am I glad you're going to the bathroom," says Courtney. "You and Scott were both sprawled out so far I couldn't get past either one of you. Let me go first, will you? You always take too long."

As I stand up I notice the scowling letter writer looking around the plane. Our eyes meet briefly. Then suddenly he reaches for his flight bag and sets up his table.

LOWELL
Wednesday, July 31, morning
Aboard 747

7

To Whom It May Concern,
        This girl keeps watching me. I wish she'd mind her own business. . . .

Dear. Mr. Stringham,
        About the business of handling the literary magazine next year, I thank you for appointing me as editor but feel I must disclaim this honor. . . .

Dear Jill,
        It isn't fair. It isn't fair. Why can't I die, too? . . .

JANE
Wednesday, July 31, morning
Heathrow Airport, London

8

Scott hunkers behind Courtney and rat-a-tats her shoulders with two index fingers. A drummer working his instruments. "I can tell this is going to be a great trip, more or less," he says.

Courtney giggles.

I make a face to get her attention, but she ignores me.

Scott quits drumming but holds the same two fingers in the air while he does a little dance step. Drummer. Dancer. A versatile performer.

"Interesting people and stuff like that," Scott says.

Courtney flashes her sunniest cheerleader smile.

We have all claimed our bags and are standing in the lines for customs inspection. Court and Scott are in the

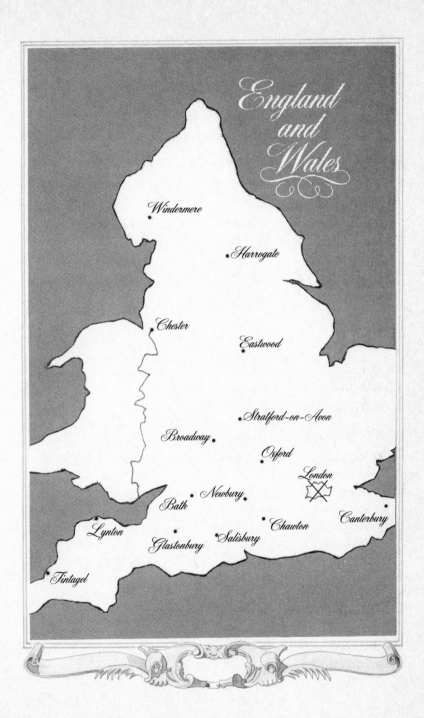

middle of my line, but for reasons of my own I'm lagging to the rear.

"Courtney," I call in a hoarse whisper.

She turns her back to me.

"Courtney," I call louder. "Come here."

She looks at me at last, but she also frowns. "What do you want?"

"Come here," I repeat.

Court rolls her eyes at the ceiling and walks close enough so I can talk softly. "You promised to stay with me," I remind her.

"Well, come on up the line with us." She smiles sweetly to the bearded man in front of me. "This is my little sister. You won't mind if she stands in line with us, will you?"

The man shrugs.

I grab her and move farther away so he can't hear. "It's all I asked, and you promised. Not to tell anyone about me and to stay with me through customs."

"Dad says they never bother people in the green lanes who have nothing to declare. Anyhow, who cares if you've got a few needles in your bag?"

"I care."

"Well, the customs people won't," she informs me. "They'll know the difference between insulin and heroin. Anyhow, all you've got to do is show them Dr. Lieberman's letter."

"It's not the customs people I care about," I remind her in a whisper. "It's the other kids."

"Oh honestly, Jane. It's not a sin to have diabetes."

"No, but for once in my life I want to be treated like everyone else. Just for once. I don't want people to think I'm a weirdo."

"No one said being sick makes you a weirdo. What makes you a freak is trying to hide a little thing like diabetes from the rest of the world."

I don't answer that, even though I know Patty Popular would have lots more trouble handling shots twice a day and regular trips to the doctor and special diets and unwanted sympathy (especially unwanted sympathy!) than I do. What I say is, "You promised to help me."

Court doesn't say anything, but if looks could kill, I wouldn't have to wait for diabetes to do me in.

"You promised *Mom*," I remind her.

She sends me that poisonous look for another second or two. Then she sighs and heads back up the line to claim her suitcase. By the time she reaches it, a new expression covers her face. "Excuse me, please, Scott," she says loud enough for everyone in the entire airport to hear, "but my sweet little sister needs me to baby-sit her."

I feel the color rising in my cheeks. But at least I won't be alone if the customs inspector opens my bag. And I make Court wait at the end of the line until all the other kids with green tapes on their luggage have left the room.

JANE
Wednesday, July 31, morning
Tour bus, London

9

I feel a bony elbow in my ribs. "You're a pushee," says the girl who's sitting next to me. Her name tag says she's Lucy Beth Ostermiller from Chicago.

We're riding on the top of a double-decker red tour bus, bumping through airport traffic toward the highway.

"Huh?" I say.

"Pushee," she repeats. "Every teenager who goes to Europe is either a pusher or a pushee. Count on it."

She's a tall, skinny girl with a nose that hooks slightly to the left. A ball of frizzy hair perches on her head like a lemon-colored Brillo pad.

I study the purple flight bag on her lap (everyone else has put their carry-ons on the floor), worrying that she's trying to sell me coke or something. No one has ever tried to sell me cocaine, and I don't know how to refuse and still act cool. "How do you figure I'm a pushee?"

"Easy." She slides her glasses back up her long nose. They're so dirty I wonder how she sees through them.

I feel my heart doing strange things. Did this girl see the medical kit in my purse? She could be a blabbermouth. Or a blackmailer. Maybe both. *"How?"* I demand.

"I just know these things."

Wondering how to deal with this, I look out the window at a woman who's repacking her suitcase right on the sidewalk. Then I take a breath and turn back to Lucy Beth. "You don't know anything about me."

"Yes, I do. I watched you on the plane and again in the meeting we just had at the airport. Everyone else talked back and forth. But you sat off by yourself pretending to read your Monarch Notes. Pushers don't read Monarch Notes unless they're cramming for a test. You're a pushee."

I open my mouth to say something but can't think what it is.

She unzips the flight bag and shuffles through bottles, dirty tissues, hairy brushes and combs. Scrunge piles up on her lap as she continues to search.

"None of this is an accident, you know. All of us are here either because we pushed our parents to send us to Europe or they pushed us to come." A faint smile lights her face. "There it is. Want some?" She holds out a package of bubble gum.

I shake my head. Even if Dr. Lieberman let me chew bubble gum, which he doesn't, I don't think I'd want any from that flight bag.

She shrugs, unwraps a ball for herself, and pops it into her mouth. Then she scoops the papers and scruffy brushes from her lap and stuffs them back into her purple bag. "Everything we do in life is related to pushing contests. You didn't want to come to Europe, but you're so used to being pushed around that you came quietly when your parents suggested it."

My father would be surprised to hear that. I picture him and Courtney back home in Atherton. *"But I can't afford it this summer, Court. I took a real drubbing on that real estate deal, and my quarterly taxes are due."*

"Oh, Daddy. Jane will be so disappointed. And I've told all my friends that we're going. I won't be able to face them."

"It wasn't like that at all," I say.

"Don't apologize. Do you want to know why I'm here? Because my mother wasn't chosen for Junior League again this year, and she'll be forty before you know it. It's time to sublimate by buying me something that Julia Evershed can't buy for her daughter. Mainly because Julia Evershed doesn't have a daughter."

"Who's Julia Evershed?" I ask.

"Julia Evershed is our next-door neighbor who belongs to Junior League and rubs my mother's nose in it. The first year after the Eversheds moved in and Mother wasn't chosen to join Junior League, she wrote an essay for me so I'd win a hundred-dollar prize and get my picture in the newspaper. The next year she wasn't chosen she enrolled me at Carrington Academy, even though it meant she had to sell my grandmother's jewelry to pay for my tuition. This year when she wasn't chosen for Junior League she decided to send me to Jolly Old England for three weeks with Old Hen. Don't tell *me* about pushees."

I'm not telling her about pushees. She's telling me. She's also dropping names of people I don't know. "Who's Old Hen?" I ask.

"Old Henry Phillips. Our leader on this summer idyll. Also warden of the place where they keep me locked up. At least during the school year. It tells you a lot about him to realize that I'm the only one of his actual students that he was able to recruit for this outing. All the rest of you innocents come from places where Carrington Academy is nothing but an ad in a slick-papered magazine."

I swallow, wondering how I'm supposed to answer.

Lucy Beth pushes her glasses back up her nose and squints at my name tag. " 'Jane Johnson, Atherton, California.' Where's Atherton, anyway?"

"Nothern California. Near San Francisco," I explain.

"No kidding? You're really from Sin City?" She looks around to see who's listening. "I know all about San Francisco," she tells me.

"Have you been there?" I ask.

"No, but don't think I don't know about the world just because I live in Old Hen's mausoleum. I'm not like some of those other infants at Carrington," she says.

"You're not?"

"Do you know what makes me different from the others? I read a lot." She leans closer. "*Cosmopolitan. Playgirl. The National Enquirer.* I know everything about San Francisco. You'll find out."

"You can't always believe what you read in the media," I tell her, parroting my father. "Anyhow, we're not that close to San Francisco. Atherton is closer to Palo Alto. You know. Stanford University."

Lucy Beth nods appreciatively. "Yes, I know. College towns are wonderfully bizarre. You don't need to tell me about college towns. A city between San Francisco and a college town is exactly *the* place to live. People in Atherton must see lots of action."

I think about my parents' idea of action. Running down to the club for a game of tennis or a round of golf. Maybe a few laps in our own pool. "Listen, Lucy Beth, you've got the wrong idea about Northern California."

"Don't call me Lucy Beth," she says. "My name is Teresa." She relaxes back in her seat and works the wad of bubble gum in her mouth. At last she sticks out her tongue and begins to blow. The bubble grows bigger and bigger until it bursts.

"Your name tag says 'Lucy Beth Ostermiller,' " I point out.

"Oh that!" Teresa fans the air with a limp hand and then goes to work picking the gum from her face. "Lucy Beth is just the name my parents call me. My real name is Teresa. Do you know what I'm going to do after I've been to all the places I want to see in this world and have tried all the things I want to do? I'm going to repent and become a nun. A self-sacrificing nun who lives in a fly-infested country and saves orphans from disease and starvation. Like Mother Teresa. Maybe they'll even make me a saint."

I've never met anyone before who wanted to become a nun. My only friends who are religious go to the Episcopal church or the synogogue. "Are you a Catholic?" I ask.

"Not yet," she says, "but that doesn't matter because I haven't repented yet anyway. I'm going to be a nun, all right. Count on it. You ought to consider a religious vocation, too, Jane. Surrendering to Jesus is a good profession for pushees."

I nod. Not because I agree with her especially, but because I can't think of anything to say.

"Your name isn't right, though," she tells me. "No offense, but you'll never be promoted to saint with a name like Jane Johnson. Too colorless. Too American and ordinary."

"Nuns are supposed to be colorless," I argue.

She hasn't heard me. "You need a name with mystique. Something foreign-sounding."

"How about Jane of Arc?" I suggest. A feeble attempt at humor.

Teresa doesn't smile. "Something like Bernadette. Yes. That's it. I'm going to call you Bernadette." She extends her hand to shake mine. "Well, Bernadette, I'm glad to know you. We pushees have to stick together. There aren't too many of us on this tour, you know." She tips her head toward Scott and Courtney, who are huddled together two rows ahead of us, in the very front of the bus. "Those two, for example, are both pushers. Their Great Summer Romance won't last because neither one of them will ever give an inch. They'll just keep trying to push each other until one of them decides the contest isn't worth the struggle. Count on it."

Dr. Phillips puffs up the bus stairs then, followed by Sylvia and a tour guide in a red uniform. Last comes the Scowler. Our eyes meet briefly. Mine embarrassed. His intense and piercing, like a snake's. Quickly he turns and stumbles toward the back of the bus.

Why does he always catch me staring at him? My heart skips. Embarrassment only? Or fear?

Teresa pokes me in the ribs. "That one's a pushee, though. He hates being on this trip even worse than we do. But I don't advise you to try to make friends with him. He's a schizo if I ever saw one."

"Okay, friends," Dr. Phillips shouts. "I'm glad you're all sitting on the top deck where you can see better. Our guide until we reach the hotel is named Mary. She'll tell you about the sights as we pass them."

Mary swishes down the aisle, sharing her scent of "Babe" with everyone and wiggling her round behind. She's pretty and knows it, like Court. Not much older than Court, either. Nineteen maybe. She perches on a ledge in the front of the bus, facing the rest of us. She's so close to Scott that her silky knees almost rub against his blue jeans. Reaching for a microphone near her shoulder, she smiles at the heir to Beef and Bun.

"Well, I suppose you've all figured out that this thing-y we've just left is the airport," she giggles.

I conclude that Mary's commentary will be less than brilliant. Tuning out her mouse-sized voice, I study England on my own.

Not too unusual at first. A few pleasant meadows and country houses that might be anywhere. Then a rain-washed suburb with gray houses that match the sky. Lace curtains at the windows are all that say this isn't California.

The bus turns sharply on a street lined with banks, small offices, and drab shops. "Ooh," squeals Mary, losing her balance. "Someone catch me. I'm falling."

Scott is happy to oblige. They smile warmly at each other, nose to nose, before he lets her go.

Courtney turns angrily and stares out the window.

Well, that's the way life is, Big Sister. No one wins all the time. Not even you.

I feel an elbow in my ribs. "What did I tell you?" says Teresa. "This tour's Big Romance won't last as long as Old Hen's anecdotes about his famous English ancestors. Count on it."

LOWELL
Wednesday, July 31, 11:30 a.m.
Hotel, London

10

Dear Dad,
Just because they caught me the first time doesn't mean that I still won't go home. Dr. Phillips knew what I was planning and watched me at the airport. Stayed with me every minute while we claimed our luggage. He thinks he's really clever. . . .

Dear Chris,
It wasn't very clever of you to get pregnant. I'll never accept either one of you. Your stupid baby is no relative of mine. . . .

Dear Dr. Cline,
Relative to my headaches. I tell you I need that prescription! I didn't sleep at all last night. And I feel a new pain coming on right now. They start in the back of my neck and in a few hours spread to the left side of my forehead and pound, pound, pound. . . .

Dear Jill,
I want to pound the walls. Break something. I hate you for dying and leaving me. Why can't I die, too? . . .

"Remember, friends, it's for your own good," says Scott, mimicking Dr. Phillips.

"Buddy system!" snorts Courtney. "Have you ever heard of anything so barfy?"

We're sitting in the snack bar of the hotel—Scott, Courtney, the Scowler, and I—discussing the latest meeting with Dr. Phillips. Anyhow, Scott and Courtney are discussing. The Scowler and I are busy trying not to look at each other.

I have, however, managed a quick peek at his name tag. He's Lowell Stevens from Scottsdale, Arizona, which means he's the person assigned to the scrapbook committee with me. (Won't that be your basic death by inches, though?) I've also noticed that if he could wipe that surly expression from his face, which I'm sure he can't, and stop using controlled substances, which I'm sure he won't, he might be better-looking than Scott.

"If you stay with your buddy, you won't panic when you get separated from the group," Scott says, continuing with his impersonation of Our Leader. "It isn't always possible for forty-two people to stay together, so concentrate on staying with your buddy."

"My buddy, my buddy," sings Court in an off-key rendition of the old song. "I wonder how he thinks up all his scuzzy rules."

"He must think we're too helpless to hail a taxi by ourselves," says Scott between noisy slurps of soup. "He treats us like idiots, more or less."

Court flashes her Golden Girl smile toward Lowell and then addresses Scott. "Well, at least your roommate is someone almost your own age. You don't have to baby-sit a fourteen-year-old sister."

Lowell's hand, which is on its way to the plate of rolls, misses the target and knocks over his Pepsi. Both hands shake as he sets it upright, and if I hadn't already noticed his bloodshot eyes and figured out what they mean, I'd think that he's more depressed by this conversation than I am.

Even though I'm not exactly a fan of Lowell's, I don't think Court should bring him into our family squabbles. "Listen," I tell her, "I'm not crazy about the idea of sticking with you, either. But at least it's only for a week. Next week we don't have to stick with our roommates. We can start choosing our own buddies. And believe me"—I pause and send an ugly look that includes both Court and Scott— "I won't choose either one of you."

"Oh darn!" she wails and collapses into helpless giggles against Scott's sweatshirt.

For no reason I'm reminded of that old definition of the pessimist and the optimist. The pessimist sees a glass and thinks of it as half empty. The optimist sees the same glass and thinks of it as half full. I see the first week of this three-week trip and know that the seven days I'll be chained to this Fun Foursome will be the longest seven days of the whole tour.

Lowell must be thinking something similar because without eating his soup or his lettuce and tomato salad or any of his unspilled Pepsi, he puts his napkin on the table and stands up. "Excuse me. I have to do something before we meet the bus."

My mouth hangs open as I watch him head for the door. Then suddenly I chase after him and grab his arm. I can't believe what I'm doing, but I do it anyhow.

"Listen," my ears tell me I'm saying. My brain tells my tongue to shut up, but the darn thing just keeps on talking. "I've been looking forward to this trip for five months, and I'm not going to let anyone spoil it for me. Not Courtney or Scott or you either. With the buddy system we're stuck with and the way Court and Scott hang all over each other, you and I are going to be paired off for the next seven days. So we might as well be friends. Besides, we're both assigned to the scrapbook committee. Just the two of us." My tongue has run out of things to say, and I stand there shaking and feeling stupid. "Anyhow, I'm Jane Johnson from Atherton, California," I add lamely.

Before he can suggest I stuff it, Teresa walks by and socks me on the arm. "Don't tell *me* that the buddy system is the only form of torture that Old Hen has in store for us. I've lived in Torquemada's dungeon for a year now, and I know what he's capable of. He's got worse things in mind, Bernadette. Count on it." She turns to Lowell and includes him in the warning. "This is only the beginning. You'll find out."

As she leaves, Lowell squints at me. A speck under his microscope. "Bernadette? I thought your name was Jane Johnson."

"Don't mind her," I say. I'm trying to keep this conversation light, but my unfamiliar voice betrays me. "She hallucinates a bit. A result of all those tortures at Carrington Academy."

Lowell is not amused by my joke. "Torturers are everywhere. People we love the most torture us the worst."

He walks off.

Well. So much for my second attempt to make friends with Mr. Halloween.

LOWELL
Wednesday, July 31, 1:45 p.m.
Hotel, London

12

Dear Jill,
   I liked watching after you. Don't you understand? I liked doing it. You had no right to die.

There's a girl on this tour who follows me all over. So how do you feel about that? . . .

To Whom It May Concern,
    Jane Johnson. Not a dynamite name. . . .

JANE
Saturday, August 3, 3:20 p.m.
Hampton Court, near London

13

Dr. Phillips' umpteenth great-grandfather was a courtier to King Henry VIII, and Henry Phillips was personally named after the second Tudor king. He told us about it Wednesday at the City of London Museum. He told us about it Thursday at the Tower of London. He told us about it Friday at the British Museum and again as we fed the pigeons underneath Lord Nelson's statue in Trafalgar Square. Today he's telling us for the fifth time at Hampton Court, just outside London, "the largest and most beautiful palace in England."

"Friends, you may be interested to know that my own ancestor that I've told you about lived here at Hampton Court between 1535 and 1537. After Anne Boleyn was executed, it was his job to go around the palace and supervise the removal of all decorations which had previously been erected in her honor."

Kids like Courtney and Scott pretend to yawn and fall asleep standing up, right here on the walkway outside the palace. Others talk or eat candy bars or load their cameras with film.

Sylvia, however, smiles sweetly at her husband and bobs her head up and down, urging him to go on.

He does.

"Some people say that my ancestor was still loyal to

Anne and believed that she was innocent of adultery, which Henry accused her of. At any rate, my ancestor failed to remove two of the ornaments of the palace which had been erected to Anne. If you'll look above your heads you'll see one of them on the ceiling—a circle bearing the initials *H* and *A*, which stand for Henry and Anne." He points with the black umbrella he always carries, even though it hasn't rained since our first day in England.

Court lifts her head off Scott's shoulder. "Where?"

"There," says Scott, pointing. "The circle on the right."

"I think Henry the Eighth was a scuzzy king," Court announces. "Imagine beheading all those wives."

Old Hen seems pleased that Courtney is finally paying attention and addresses her directly. "Henry the Eighth married six women, but he only beheaded two of them. Does anyone know who they were?" He turns toward me, probably because I'm the only one who ever listens to his lectures. "Jane?"

"Well," I stammer, "Anne Boleyn was one."

"That's right," says Dr. Phillips. "Who knows the other one?" No hands are raised, so he picks on someone he knows. "Lucy Beth?"

Teresa, who has already made herself a new name tag (we have to wear them for a week) and has told everyone (including Dr. Phillips) that she won't answer to any name but Teresa, nonchalantly sticks out her tongue and blows a bubble that covers her face.

Over the rims of his glasses Dr. Phillips glares at her pink bubble, then turns to someone else. "Lowell?"

Standing off by himself, the Scowler mumbles to the tops of his Pumas. "Catherine Howard."

"Who?" says Dr. Phillips. "Speak up so everyone can hear."

"Catherine Howard," Lowell repeats. His voice blasts strangely. A faulty cassette tape turned on too loud.

"That's right," says Old Hen. "Do you know what happened to the rest of Henry's wives?"

Lowell clears his throat and sticks his thumbs in the pockets of his jeans to study a gray spider skittering over the concrete. "Katharine of Aragon was divorced. Anne Boleyn was beheaded. Jane Seymour died. Anne of Cleves was divorced. Catherine Howard was beheaded. Catherine Parr survived Henry."

Sylvia rushes to him, beaming. "That's wonderful, Lowell. *I* couldn't recite all those names so quickly."

Lowell meets her gaze briefly before staring back at the ground. "It's just an old mnemonic device that my— that someone I used to know taught me. Divorced, beheaded, died, divorced, beheaded, survived."

Coquettishly Sylvia takes his arm and draws him back to the group. She looks at Lowell as she speaks but talks loudly enough for all of us to hear. "Did you know that two of Henry's wives are supposed to haunt this palace? Jane Seymour occupies the Queen's Staircase. And Catherine Howard walks back and forth through the Haunted Gallery."

"Ghosts!" Courtney squeals.

"For neat!" says Karen Kemper, a girl from Omaha.

"In tune!" Scott agrees.

Wearing shorts and high heels, Teresa *clip-clops* up to Dr. Phillips, a rainbow of colored bracelets rattling on her wrist. Now that she's on leave from her brown Carrington uniform, she exercises genuine flair in the way she dresses. "No kidding?" she says. "This place is actually haunted?"

Old Hen nods proudly, as if he has conjured up Jane and Catherine personally. "That's what some of the guides around here claim. So I don't expect you to come inside if you're afraid. Those of you who don't want to meet any of Henry's wives can wait for us right here." He ducks his head and points with his ever-present umbrella. "The rest of you can come this way."

For once, everyone follows him eagerly. Everyone but Sylvia and Lowell, who chit-chat privately.

Straining to overhear, I notice blonde fuzz above

Sylvia's upper lip, which I suspect she tries to hide with bleach. For no reason, I feel depressed. What's it to me if an old married lady makes friends with Mr. Disagreeable? Who the heck cares if one of the other kids on this tour knows more about British history than I do? What difference does it make to anyone if I don't know what *mnemonic* means and don't even have the foggiest idea of how to look it up in the dictionary?

LOWELL
Saturday, August 3, 9:45 p.m.
Hotel, London

14

To Whom It May Concern,
    That Jane Johnson's still watching me. Why? Does Dr. Phillips know I'm still planning to go home? . . .

Dear Chris,
    You'll never take her place. You'll never take anyone's place. . . .

Dear Dr. Cline,
    You sadist. I've had a headache every day since the funeral. You could refill that prescription if you wanted to. . . .

Dear Jill,
    You want to know something? Divorced, beheaded, died, divorced, beheaded, survived. That isn't just about Henry's wives. . . .

JANE
Tuesday, August 6, 7:05 a.m.
Hotel, London

15

Scott drums on the tablecloth with two index fingers. *Tap-a-tap-tap-tap.*

"If Lowell doesn't hurry, there won't be any food left," Courtney complains.

Scott shrugs and picks up his knife and fork to try a new sound. *Thump-a-thump-thump-thump.*

The three of us are sitting at a table in one of the restaurants on the second floor of our hotel. It's a big room, full of noisy tourists waiting for various tours. Our group is scattered around the south side of the room at tables spread with white cloths.

"He's such a *loser*," says Courtney, talking in italics as she usually does. "It's absolutely *scuzzy* being chained to a loser."

With so many people lined up in the foyer until tables are vacated, I'm feeling a little guilty sitting here not eating. But strangely enough, I hear myself defending Lowell. "Listen, he probably isn't too excited about being chained to the three of us, either. I know I'll be happy when we can start choosing our own buddies."

Happy is the understatement of the week. I'm counting the days (1), hours (24), and/or minutes (1,440) until Wednesday morning when Dr. Phillips unfetters me from this double date with the Adorable Duo and Mr. Ice Sculpture. Except for the brief exchange we had about my name (which doesn't exactly count), Lowell Stevens has said exactly four words to me of his own accord: *Please pass the salt.* So sitting next to him at meals and on bus rides isn't your basic picnic. Up until now those bus rides have been fairly short. Just here and there through London. But in less than an hour we leave for Canterbury on the first lap of our long tour of the rest of Britain. For self-preservation I've packed my carry-on with armaments—about 4 million books and pamphlets—so I can pretend I'm too busy to talk to him anyhow. I'm also wishing I hadn't laughed at Brenda when she urged me to take a course in Transcendental Meditation.

Court rolls her eyes at me, and Scott continues drumming with his invisible rock group. *PING* goes his empty water glass. *Thump-a-thump-thump-PING-thump-a-thump-thump-PING*.

"He's *always* late," Court says. "Why is he *always* late?"

Scott sets down his silverware and shrugs again. "Beats me. Am I my buddy's keeper?"

Either the witticism or the end of the drumming cheers Court up. Giggling, she falls against Scott's shoulder. "Oh, you're so *fun-ny!*"

Something wipes the smile off her face. She sits up abruptly. "Well, it's about time," she whispers.

As Lowell walks toward us, she turns into her All-American Teenager self again and flashes him a smile. "Hi, Lowell. We've been waiting for you."

Lowell sets down his own armaments (a pile of books and tablets) on the empty chair, and we inch toward the breakfast buffet, which is already crowded with a busload of tourists hurrying to meet another bus schedule.

"Continental breakfast!" says a fat man in plaid walking shorts. "You call this food?"

Scott grins in the man's direction. No one on our tour is crazy about "Continental breakfast" either, especially Scott.

Old Hen has encouraged us with descriptions of the "genuine English breakfasts" we'll be served at other hotels on our travels. But for now we're still at our first hotel where "Continental buffet" consists of canned fruit juice that tastes like vinegar plus rust, coffee or tea, hard rolls or croissants, and assorted cold cereals. The others dive for the croissants (Scott takes four) and the mini-cartons of jam, but I help myself to a bowl of Alpen—partly because I don't mind Alpen too much and partly because I know Dr. Lieberman wouldn't approve of a diet of bread and jam for breakfast.

Scott sees me. "You've taken that stuff every morning. You don't really like it, do you? It looks like dried turtle eggs plus a few dead beetles."

Court giggles.

I stare at my bowl, wondering if I want to eat Alpen again or not.

Unexpectedly Lowell takes an empty bowl and pours himself some of the famous European cereal. "I think it looks good," he tells Scott. "I'm going to try some, too."

I'm wondering what to make of that when Court pours herself a bowlful, too. "Might as well try it. There's not much else."

Scott shrugs. "Why not?" he says and gets a bowl.

Back at the table Lowell is the first to speak. "This isn't bad, Jane."

Four words. To me. We have just doubled our communication.

Scott says nothing, but eats with enthusiasm, palming the bowl with his left hand about five inches from his mouth and shoveling athletically with his right. Your basic feeding time in the gorilla cage. "It is good, more or less," he admits. "I think I'll have some more."

As Scott stands up and heads toward the buffet table, Lowell watches closely, the hint of a smile playing about his mouth.

Yes. I've decided for sure. Lowell is handsomer than Scott. Definitely.

JANE
Tuesday, August 6, 7:32 a.m.
Hotel, London

16

Before we can go down the escalator to the ground floor where the bus meets us, we have to wait in the second-floor lobby for our tour to be called. No kidding. This hotel doesn't permit loitering on the ground level.

Kids from our group buzz around the lobby among gray-haired people from other tours. Most of the people are standing. Not enough seats for everyone.

I do see one empty seat, though, and wonder if I dare take it. On a sofa next to the place where Lowell is sitting.

Maybe he's going to be friendly now. He did speak to me at breakfast. I walk closer.

On the floor his books and tablets are scattered, and I relax a little as I read the title of a paperback. *Murder in the Cathedral* by T. S. Eliot. That should give us something to talk about—even though he's reading the real play, not just the Monarch Notes.

Suddenly he looks in my direction. But he doesn't see me. His eyes stare over my shoulder.

Then he picks up a tablet and begins to write.

LOWELL
Tuesday, August 6, 7:35 a.m.
Hotel, London

17

Dear Dad,
Scott had a phone call from his dad this morning. I suppose you're too busy enjoying yourself in Bermuda to phone me. Or even write. Not that it matters. . . .

JANE
Tuesday, August 6, 8:07 a.m.
Tour bus to Canterbury

18

"You want the window?" Lowell asks.

Four more words.

Eight words in one hour.

Twelve words altogether. More than deserved for your basic dull person who is unhealthy besides.

"Well?" he says.

"Why don't we take turns?" I suggest. "You go first." I step back, wondering why I said that. I really want the window myself. The whole ride.

I wish we were back on the double-decker bus that our tour provided for London driving. Two people could see out of those upper windows, with hardly any trouble at all.

Except for its color (red), this bus is just like a Trailways back home. Narrow aisles. Not enough leg room. Skimpy overhead storage. All but these two seats are taken, and the air presses its dankness on your skin and up your nostrils. (Old Hen can use his umbrella today!) Without thanking me, Lowell glides into the seat by the window and puts his books on the floor. Then I sit down too, feeling like a squashed cherry in an overpacked bottle.

"Well, friends," comes a familiar voice over the microphone, "We're all aboard."

The engine coughs, the gears grind, and we rumble through the covered loading zone and out to the street.

Leaning back against rough upholstery, I smell the sour odors of stale tobacco (If food is illegal on British buses, why are cigarettes allowed?) and human perspiration. I close my eyes and breathe deeply, grateful that I remembered to take a Dramamine.

"The trip to Canterbury will take us just over an hour

in this nice air-conditioned bus, friends," Dr. Phillips tells us through his microphone. "But it used to take pilgrims lots longer than that."

"Hey, man, I thought the Pilgrims went to Plymouth Rock," a kid shouts out, and I recognize the voice of Merrill Bickerstaff from Iowa. In spite of the name tags we've been wearing for six days, I haven't memorized the names of all eight guys and all thirty-two girls who have come on this tour. But Merrill Bickerstaff is the sort of person you notice right away. He's six feet eight with carrot-colored hair, and he's always bumping into things. Like the busboy in London, who was carrying about two million dishes.

Old Hen clears his throat through the mike. "Good comment, Merrill. Good comment." Only yesterday Dr. Phillips told Merrill publicly that his name wasn't "man," but I guess he's decided to overlook that today. "The word *pilgrims*," continues Old Hen in that headmaster voice he uses when he's trying to explain things, "sometimes refers to the English colonists who settled in Massachusetts."

He pauses, waiting for us to urge him to go on. No one does, but he continues anyhow. "But it also refers to people like us who are traveling to worship at a holy shrine."

"Not me, man," says Merrill. "I ain't that kind of pilgrim."

"Maybe you don't plan to worship," says Dr. Phillips, "but you *are* traveling to a holy shrine. Canterbury Cathedral was the site of a famous martyrdom in 1170. Does anyone know who was killed there and why?"

Cripes, I know the answer to that. I've read *A Proud Taste for Scarlet and Miniver* five times, after all. I'm sure Lowell knows the answer, too, since he's carrying *Murder in the Cathedral* around with him. But neither of us is famous for volunteering information when we're not called on.

Old Hen tips his head to one side, waiting for the answer. He's standing in the front of the bus, and I'm on practically the last row. But I can see him well enough from the aisle seat to decide he really does look like a hen when he stands that way. "Well, friends," he urges, "does anyone know?"

Is Lowell going to answer? I turn to read his expression, but he's staring out the window at a hedgerow standing sentinel between the narrow road and someone's farm.

"Tch, tch," clucks Dr. Phillips through the mike, even sounding like a hen. "Thomas à Becket, the archbishop of Canterbury, was murdered in his very own cathedral. You'll see the exact spot where he was surprised during his prayers. People have been making religious pilgrimages there ever since, for more than eight hundred years."

Old Hen goes on talking, but I feel this punch on my arm and hear the rattle of Teresa's colored bracelets.

Stretching across the aisle, she gives me a speech of her own. "Don't say I didn't tell you about the rewards of a religious life. After you're made a saint, the church declares the exact spot you died a shrine, and people come there to worship for hundreds of years."

"Yeah, but you have to be martyred first," I argue. "I don't think I'd make a very good martyr. I wouldn't die heroically, like Thomas à Becket."

Teresa jerks her head so that dangly earrings swing back and forth. "Well, I will."

"Lots of luck. It hurts to be stabbed."

"It's fast, though," Teresa says.

"Maybe, but I'd just as soon die naturally."

Teresa brushes the air between us with a limp hand. "Dying naturally isn't all it's cracked up to be. I know all about dying naturally. My grandma died naturally, and it took her exactly four years and seven months—in this bizarre nursing home with demented old people walking around in their underwear and slobbering. Don't tell me about dying naturally."

"Martyrdom isn't so wonderful, either," I say. "That's why people who go through it are made saints."

"Well, I don't plan to suffer when I'm martyred,"

Teresa replies. "I won't fight my attackers, so I'll die quickly. Anyway, it's not going to happen until I'm eighty-five or eighty-six. And by then I'll have rescued lots of starving orphans and won the Nobel Peace Prize. You'll see. And you'll be sorry if you haven't decided to become a nun, too. Because that's the best thing you can do with your life after you've repented." She pinches her mouth into a little circle and sits back primly in her seat. For no reason I look over at Lowell, who has taken a tablet and envelope from the floor and is writing another of his interminable letters to that girl friend of his. (I know it's a girl because he always covers the paper with his left hand.)

I wonder if he heard what Teresa and I were talking about. For that mattter, I wonder if he's heard any of Dr. Phillips' famous lecture about Thomas à Becket and his murder in Canterbury Cathedral.

LOWELL
Tuesday, August 6, 8:45 a.m.
Tour bus to Canterbury

19

Dear Jill,
  Did you suffer much? . . .

Dear Dr. Cline,
  You quack. . . .

A sharp elbow clobbers me right between the shoulder blades. "I forgive you, Bernadette," says Teresa.

"Huh?" I say. I'm trying to take a picture of the spot where Thomas à Becket was murdered, and every time I get my camera in focus, some tourist walks into my viewfinder. It's been five days since Dr. Phillips appointed Lowell and me to handle the scrapbook together, and so far the committee members haven't exchanged forty words, much less talked about their assignment. I figure it's up to me to take all the important pictures, and right now I'm too busy concentrating on that to follow Teresa's weird logic.

"I forgive you," she repeats. "It just wouldn't be saintly of me to stand right here by this actual spot where Thomas à Becket fell to his noble death with malice in my heart for a fellow pushee."

I don't answer, waiting for a girl in a red sweater to get out of my view.

Teresa slugs me again in the same place, even harder. "I forgive you," she says louder.

"Cripes," I say, rubbing my back, "if that's the way you treat people you forgive, I'm sure glad you're not mad at me."

"Well, don't think I *wouldn't* be mad at you if we were standing on any other spot in the whole United Kingdom."

The girl in the red sweater moves out of the way, and I refocus. *Click.*

"But on England's most hallowed ground, where pilgrims have walked with bleeding feet for more than eight hundred years, I forgive you for saying that martyrdom isn't wonderful and you'd rather die a natural death."

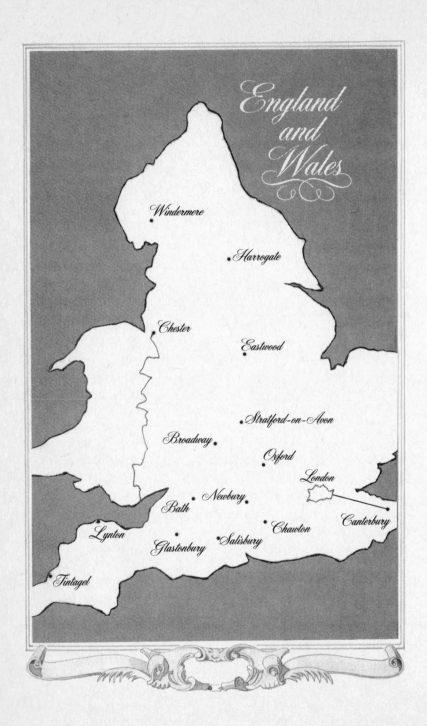

England and Wales

Windermere

Harrogate

Chester

Eastwood

Stratford-on-Avon

Broadway

Oxford

London

Newbury

Bath

Canterbury

Lynton

Chawton

Glastonbury   Salisbury

Tintagel

I'm completely nonplussed. I can't even come up with a sarcastic *Thanks*.

"But don't think because I forgive you, Bernadette, that you can get away with that attitude forever. You'll never get anywhere, religiously speaking, if you don't improve your mental attitude. You'll see."

She spins around and *clip-clops* on teetery high heels up the steps to the main part of the church.

I watch the lemon-colored hair (even frizzier than usual in this damp weather), the straight set of her spine, the bold-patterned silk blouse with its splashes of purple and pink, envying Teresa's confidence about her future. How would it be to make plans for how you were going to die at age eighty-six?

I sigh. As a rule, I don't worry too much about my illness and when or how I might die. Dr. Lieberman assures me that a cure for diabetes is on the way. Probably before I graduate from college. Possibly even before I graduate from high school. But meanwhile, I've missed out on the normal kind of life that most kids take for granted. And what if Dr. Lieberman is wrong? (He doesn't work in any of those labs. How can he know how long it will take?) What if the cure doesn't come until after I've already developed all those problems that diabetics can get? Liver ailments. Heart attacks. Blindness. Amputations. Not to mention those two kinds of spells that I've already had—diabetic comas and hypoglycemic reactions. When I have a hypoglycemic reaction (Courtney keeps reminding me), I yell at people and throw things and act like an escapee from your basic horror movie.

My cousin Paul, who had diabetes, died at seventeen, before he even graduated from high school. You don't see any church making his bed a holy shrine. But he deserves to be called a martyr if anyone does. He suffered plenty before he died.

Without even realizing when I started to cry, I taste salty tears streaming down to my chin.

Suddenly I am aware that Lowell has been standing here at Thomas à Becket's shrine, possibly for a long time. He rubs his eyes with the backs of his hands. Is he crying, too?

Our eyes meet, and for the first time he doesn't look away in anger.

LOWELL 21
Tuesday, August 6, 10:20 a.m.
Cathedral, Canterbury

To Whom It May Concern,
*   I guess I've been so busy thinking about myself that I've forgotten other people sometimes have problems, too. . . .*

Dear Dad,
*   Maybe I won't go home, after all. Why should I? It isn't as if I'm looking forward to a reunion with you. . . .*

JANE 22
Tuesday, August 6, 10:55 a.m.
Cathedral, Canterbury

Outside the huge doors the rain comes down in rivers. The sky is gray. The walkways are gray. Even the grass out there looks gray.

We're huddled inside the entrance of Canterbury Cathedral, waiting for the rain to let up. The girls are tying scarves around their heads. Some of the guys have found newspapers for protection.

"Synchronize your watches, friends," Old Hen directs.

"It's five minutes to eleven. We'll meet back at the bus at one p.m. sharp, which gives you exactly two hours and five minutes to eat and see the town. Hang on to your buddies, though. You wouldn't want to get lost in this torrent."

"Come on," Merrill Bickerstaff tells Ryan Donovan, his friend from Iowa. I've just found out that they play football together. "There's a mall over that way with lots of restaurants. I'm hungry."

They go out and jog down the path in the direction Merrill pointed. Just then a zigzag of light slashes the grayness, followed by an explosion.

"I'm not going out in that," says Karen Kemper. "I don't like lightning."

"Yes, you are," says Teresa. "You're my buddy, and Dr. Phillips said we have to stick together."

"Lightning struck my uncle's barn last summer and killed two of his horses," says Karen.

Teresa swings her limp hand in an arc. "One little barn? That's nothing. I saw a man on television who was actually struck by lightning seven times. I know all about lightning."

"This dress was a going-away present from my grand-mother," Karen argues. "It's never been washed."

"Don't apologize," says Teresa. "A little rain will make it smell good as new. Come on, we've got to stay close to Merrill and Ryan. If lightning's going to hit someone, it will get the tallest person around."

Teresa pushes Karen through the door, and, sheeplike, the others follow, heading in the direction Merrill has taken. I'm at the tail of the group, and the rain has eased to a light drizzle by the time I get outdoors.

Ah. I stop for a moment, enjoying the sweet coolness that fills the lungs. Then, giddy with what I've inhaled, I race after Courtney and Scott.

Someone grabs my arm. "Hey, let's not eat with them today," Lowell says.

I'm more than giddy. I'm drunk. I've just imagined that Lowell has asked me out to lunch. Alone.

I even talk like a drunk. "Huh?"

"Come on," he says. "Just the two of us. I'll lose my cookies if I have to eat another meal with that perpetual rhythm machine."

I look up at him, astonished at the flow of words, at his tight grip on my arm.

"Well?" he says.

My arm feels warm where he's holding it. "We're supposed to stay with Courtney and Scott. We're not supposed to go off together."

"And he eats like a cannibal. Haven't you noticed that he eats like a cannibal? He holds his fork in his fist and throws his food into his mouth."

"At least we never have to watch him for very long. He's always finished before the rest of us have even been served."

"I'm chained to him twenty-four hours a day. Do you have any idea what it's like to be chained to him twenty-four hours a day? Besides, they're as sick of us as we are of them. We'd be doing them a favor by going off by ourselves."

"What would Dr. Phillips say?" I ask, sounding like a second-grader. It occurs to me that I really don't care what Dr. Phillips would say. It occurs to me that I'm resisting the invitation because I want Lowell to like me, and I'm afraid he isn't going to when he finds out how dull I am.

"He'd probably say—" Lowell cocks his head to one side and mimics Old Hen's voice: "Friends, well, you're finally acting like friends."

I laugh. It's never occurred to me that Lowell might have a sense of humor.

He smiles back. "Come on," he urges, pulling my arm. He's taken my laughter as acceptance. Which it probably is.

"Where are we going?" I ask.

"I saw a little place over this way. Look, I promise not to ask you any personal questions—like why you were crying in the cathedral—because I don't want you to ask me any personal questions either. Okay?"

"Okay," I say.

Lowell puts his arm around me to protect me from the rain as we walk and leads me in a different direction from the one the others took. I wonder if he realizes that no boy has ever put his arm around me before.

He seems perfectly comfortable, though, as if he's done it lots of times. I guess that shouldn't surprise me, even if he's always seemed so shy. He's older than I am (sixteen, at least), and he's always writing letters to that girlfriend.

I wonder what she's like . . .

JANE
Tuesday, August 6, 1:10 p.m.
Tour bus to Chawton

23

"Darn," I say. I look frantically out of the window at the disappearing city.

"What's the matter?" Lowell asks.

We're back on the bus after eating minestrone soup and salad in a quaint little tea room, and I'm taking my turn by the window.

"I didn't get a picture of Canterbury Cathedral from the outside," I say.

Lowell shrugs. "I didn't get a picture of Thomas à Becket at his prayers."

"I'm serious," I say.

"Buy a postcard," he suggests.

"You don't understand," I say. How could anyone

understand? A picture that I've taken myself would prove that I've been here.

And I was so busy talking to Lowell in the restaurant—so busy enjoying his company—that I didn't notice it had stopped raining and that I could go back to the cathedral and take a picture.

"Try me," he says.

"Canterbury Cathedral is one of the places I've really looked forward to seeing. One of the most important places on this whole tour."

"Why?"

"Because I've read so much about it. Because Eleanor of Aquitaine has actually been there."

Lowell unbuttons his leather jacket. "Look, we're going to lots of places Eleanor has been. Salisbury Cathedral. Stonehenge."

"I know. That's why I chose this particular tour. I want to photograph them all."

"Well, you took some pictures inside Canterbury Cathedral. I saw you," he tells me. "Besides, you can't get a picture of the cathedral from outside. Not unless you have a wide-angle lens."

"Did you try?" I ask.

"Not on this trip. I didn't bring a camera."

"You came all the way to England, and you didn't bring a camera?"

"I packed in a hurry," he says.

"No one packs in too big a hurry to bring a camera. A camera is more important than a toothbrush," I argue. Then I put two and two together. "I get it. You've been to England so many times you've already photographed every square inch."

He shakes his head. "Just once."

"Then you stayed a long time."

"Ten days," he says, studying a loose button on his leather jacket. He yanks it off and puts it in the pocket of his jeans. "Someone was sick. I had to go home early."

"Who?"

"No personal questions," he says. "We promised each other. Remember?"

I wonder if his going home early had something to do with that girlfriend he writes to. If it does, maybe I'd just as soon not know about it. I slip off my shoes, curling my feet up under me on the seat, and change the subject. "If you could trade places with anyone in history, who would it be?"

"Mmm," he says, thinking. "Merlin, maybe. I've always wanted to work magic."

"That's not fair. What real person would you like to be?"

He thinks again. "Harry Truman."

"Why?" I ask.

"A country boy who made good."

Somehow Lowell doesn't strike me as a country boy. I smile. "Were you one of those little boys who always wanted to grow up to be president?"

He smiles back, warming me all over. "I don't know. Maybe. The real thing I admire about Truman was his constancy. True to his childhood sweetheart and his convictions all his life."

Yeah, Lowell's thinking about his girlfriend, all right. But I've promised not to ask him any personal questions.

He shifts in his seat so he can look straight at me. His gray eyes almost bore holes in my face, but his mouth is soft and turns up at the corners. His hair is still wet from the rain and clings in black curls to his forehead. "Who would you trade places with?"

Even though I was leading up to this question, even though I know exactly what I'd planned to say, his gaze makes me uncomfortable. I don't answer.

"Well?" he insists.

"Eleanor of Aquitaine," I say at last.

"Eleanor of Aquitaine," he snorts. "You don't have anything in common with Eleanor of Aquitaine."

"I know. That's why I'd like to trade places with her."

"Do you know that her husband, Henry II, imprisoned her fifteen years for treason?"

"She wasn't in prison," I tell him. "It was only house arrest. Anyhow, she led an interesting life even during those years. Collecting all those wonderful King Arthur legends. Eleanor was a tough lady. No one ever pushed her around. She was a real survivor."

Lowell stares at something across the aisle so I see his Roman nose in profile. For a minute I almost wonder if he's gone back into his shell again and won't talk to me. "Survival is greatly overrated," he says at last. "Take it from someone who knows. Anyhow, your sister Courtney might be suited to trade places with Eleanor of Aquitaine, but you make a better Jane. Jane Austen."

Jane Austen? I don't know anything about Jane Austen except that she wrote novels and we're on our way to see her house. I'm worried about what Lowell means, and maybe I frown a little.

He grins. Even though he has a nice smile, I sense he's laughing at me, and I don't like being laughed at. I feel my cheeks getting warm. "You must be a real Jane Austen fan. You're carrying all those Monarch Notes around."

Now I'm really blushing. I feel awful. "My English teacher gave me all those books to read, but I just can't get into them," I explain.

"Of course not," Lowell says. "No one can get into Monarch Notes. There ought to be a law against trying to get into Monarch Notes."

I bite my lip, unable to think of anything to say. Why does Lowell always know so much more than I do? I hate it when other kids know more than I do.

"Hey," Lowell says. He reaches over and squeezes my hand. "I meant it as a compliment when I said you were like Jane Austen."

JANE
Tuesday, August 6, 3:40 p.m.
Jane Austen's house, Chawton

24

By the door of Jane Austen's house grows a hydrangea bush with blooms of no particular color. The house itself is red brick with white window frames. Boxlike. Without distinction. And too near the street.

But what's inside a house tells you more about a person than the building, I decide. Maybe I'll like that better. I enter from the south into a drawing room about twenty feet square that has a prim, tidy look, staying close to Dr. Phillips to hear everything I can about Jane Austen.

The first things I hear I don't like at all.

"Well, friends, I guess you'd have to say that Jane Austen lived more in her own imagination than she did in the real world. The most interesting event of her life was her friendship with a clergyman who died before they ever became engaged. She never married or associated with the famous people of London literary life. When she wasn't writing, she spent all her time assisting her mother and sister with ordinary domestic chores. And she died in 1817 at the age of forty-two."

"Bor-ing!" says Court.

I shift the strap of my camera, studying a tiny pink flower on the wallpaper. Is that what Lowell thinks of me? That I'm boring?

We pass through a small hallway with a fireplace into another room labeled "The Parlour" but furnished to resemble a dining room. Old Hen points to a round table by the window which is so small there's no room on it to rest an arm. "That table is the one on which Jane wrote. And she never fixed this squeaking door"—he demonstrates it for us—"which leads to the stairs. Jane always

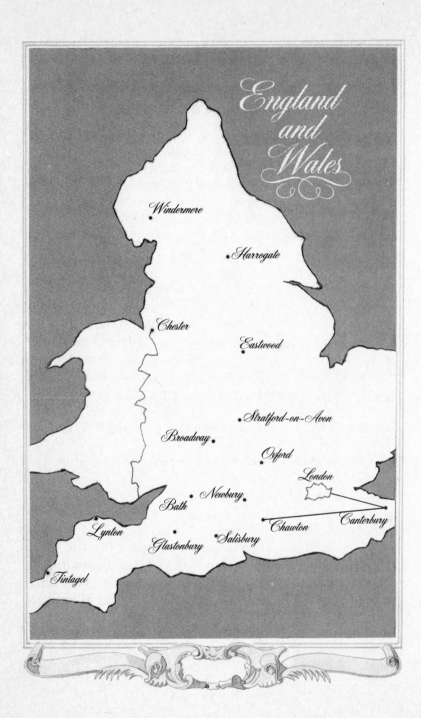

England and Wales

Windermere

Harrogate

Chester

Eastwood

Stratford-on-Avon

Broadway

Oxford

London

Newbury

Bath

Chawton

Canterbury

Lynton

Salisbury

Glastonbury

Tintagel

wanted to be warned if anyone was coming so she could hide her manuscripts."

"Hey, man, what did she write them for if she didn't want anyone to read them?" Merrill asks. "Why was she ashamed of them?"

"Yeah, what kind of stories were they?" Scott asks.

Old Hen cocks his head to one side, considering that question. "Nothing she should have been ashamed of. Satires mostly. About struggling clerical families. And mothers looking for eligible husbands for their daughters. Jane Austen tells us a lot about British life in the early nineteenth century."

Court rolls her eyes at the ceiling. "I'll bet," she whispers to Scott.

Old Hen either doesn't hear or pretends not to. He leads us up the staircase (so narrow that one person must squeeze flat against the wall if another tries to pass) to the bedrooms. The first one—Jane's—has a faded patchwork quilt hanging on the wall, and Old Hen tells us that she made it herself.

Suddenly I notice something else on the opposite wall— a painting of a woman. I rush over to see if the note hanging beside it says that this is Jane. Yes. There she is. The woman Lowell thinks I'm like.

She isn't a pretty woman. Her lips are too thin. Her nose is too long and pointed. Her neck is too thick. Except for large brown eyes (I have large brown eyes), she is very undistinguished looking.

Plain Jane Austen. Just like me.

I grow more depressed as we walk to the other bedrooms and see the pictures of Jane's brothers in their splendid military uniforms. Their lives must have been active and colorful. Like Court's. Or even like Mom's and Dad's.

I wish I'd never talked to Lowell Stevens. I wish he'd ignored me today, the way he's been ignoring me for a whole week.

He confronts me as I go back to the bus and slump down into my seat by the window. "Look, Old Hen didn't tell you anything about Jane Austen," he says. "If you want to know about her, read these."

He hands me a small package he has purchased in the house that contains three paperbacks by Jane Austen.

"How much do I owe you?" I ask. I'm not really sure I want to spend my money for three books by a boring author.

He holds out the palm of his hand. "A present. Just promise you'll read them."

"Thanks," I say. What else can I say?

"Pride and Prejudice is the best. Read that one first."

Dubiously I look at the other two books, *Emma* and *Northanger Abbey*. Not one of them contains pictures by the author, like *A Proud Taste for Scarlet and Miniver* by E. L. Konigsburg, but Lowell seems so certain that I want to start reading them right this minute that he pulls out his tablet and an envelope and begins to write.

LOWELL
Tuesday, August 6, 5:05 p.m.
Tour bus to Newbury

25

Dear Dr. Cline,

It's five o'clock, and I haven't had a headache. I've felt pretty good all day, ever since I finally broke down and bawled this morning at Canterbury Cathedral. Maybe you were right when you said my problem was that I hadn't really grieved yet for Jill. . . .

"Okay, Scott, you come with me," says Old Hen.

Excitement crackles through the bus as Scott stands up from a rear seat and prances up the aisle to join Dr. Phillips. We crowd near the windows and watch anxiously as the two of them walk from the parking lot into the hotel. This is the moment we've all been waiting for. The first mail call.

The letter of instructions we received from Dr. Phillips before we came to England contained a complete itinerary of all the places we would be staying and all the dates. But because of difficulties with mail deliveries, Dr. Phillips told us to instruct our families and friends to allow at least a week for letters and to address the earliest correspondence to our hotel in Newbury.

Well, here we are. Newbury.

As mailman for the tour, Scott's job is to go to the front desk and sort all our mail while Old Hen checks us in and gets our room assignments.

I bite my lip, hoping for at least two letters. One from Mom or Daddy. One from Brenda.

Other people must be worrying as I am because no one speaks. Catlike silence. Merrill scratches his arm. Teresa chews her fingernails. Lowell stares straight ahead at an invisible object in the front of the bus.

Time drags. I can't even get into my Jane Austen novel again.

At last they appear through the hotel door, Old Hen carrying the expected keys, Scott carrying a big bundle of white envelopes. I swallow.

"Hey, did I get anything?" Merrill calls out.

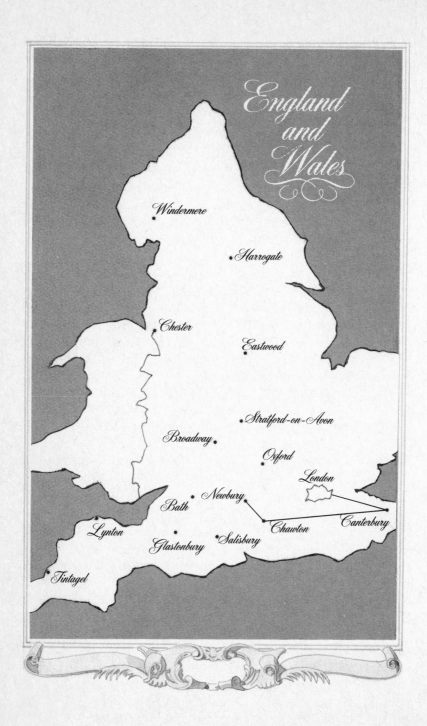

England
and
Wales

Windermere

Harrogate

Chester

Eastwood

Stratford-on-Avon

Broadway

Oxford

London

Bath   Newbury

Lynton   Chawton   Canterbury

Glastonbury   Salisbury

Tintagel

"Me first," says Ryan.

Old Hen takes the microphone. "I know you're more anxious for the mail than you are for your room assignments, friends. But it will avoid confusion if I hand out keys first."

Another wait while we go through that routine.

"All right, friends, as Scott reads your names through the mike, you can come forward to pick up your mail and go to your rooms." Old Hen grins at Scott and hands over the mike.

Scott takes it, grinning too. Tweedledee and Tweedledum. They feel they deserve the credit for all those letters that people have sent us.

"Okay," Scott begins, "you'll be glad to know that nearly everyone got letters, more or less, but Jane Johnson got the best mail."

My heart thumps. I got the best mail? Me?

"She was the only one who received a postcard," Scott continues. "And it's so good I thought you all should see it."

I feel my privacy being invaded but am afraid people will think I'm a bad sport if I protest. I lean forward.

Scott holds up one of those oversized postcards that Brenda is famous for.

Faint laughter trickles through the bus, but I'm sitting too far back to see the picture. "What is it?" I ask Lowell. "Can you see?"

Teresa hears my question and calls back an answer. "Nothing X-rated. Just a cute little boy and girl kissing each other."

Sighing, I slouch back in my seat. It could have been worse. Lots worse.

"The message is the best part, though," Scott says. "Do you all want to hear it?"

Yeahs ring out all over as my heart thumps even harder than it did before. Isn't there a federal law against reading other people's mail? Especially to a whole audience? Old

Hen should know. He specializes in rules. I look at him for support, but he's still grinning, as broadly as ever.

"*Dear Jane,*" Scott reads, then pauses for dramatic effect. "*How are all those cute guys you planned to meet? Which one did you make out with first? Write soon with all the sexy details. Life in Atherton is dull as grass this summer. Wish I were there. Brenda.*"

Everyone roars, and I laugh, too, pretending to be a good sport. But I'm really hurting inside.

What is Lowell Stevens thinking of me now?

JANE
Wednesday, August 7, 7:15 a.m.
Hotel, Newbury

27

The lobby of this hotel is as dark and silent as a Black Hole. I squirm in the bristly chair, astonished at my boldness.

I'm about to invite Lowell to be my buddy today. If he gets here before I lose my nerve.

It's Jane Austen who gave me courage. I finished *Pride and Prejudice* last night and had started *Emma* before Court got in at 3:30 a.m. from her hot date with Scott. The thing is, if Lowell thinks I'm like Jane Austen, he must like me. At least a little. Even if Jane Austen isn't your basic Loni Anderson—at least to look at—she has other things going for her. She's optimistic and wise and genteel and even funny.

Removing my shoes, I curl my legs up under me and silently practice different ways to begin:

Hi, Lowell, I've nearly finished reading Emma *already.* No.

Do you really think I'm like Jane Austen? No. Definitely not.

I love Jane Austen. Barfy, as Courtney might say.
Thank you for the fantastic books. Too gushy.

The longer I wait, the more nervous I become. Maybe this isn't such a good idea. Maybe I should grab some fruit from the buffet table and go back to my bench on the terrace to read until everyone comes to breakfast.

Footsteps startle me, and I look up. It's only Court.

"Have you seen Scott?" she asks.

"No."

"How long have you been here?"

"Nearly half an hour," I say.

"Well, come to breakfast with me. I'm starving."

"I'm not hungry," I lie.

"Have you already eaten?" she asks.

"No."

"Well, you better get something right now. You had your shot a long time ago. You could go into you-know-what."

She means hypoglycemic reaction, of course. Diabetics are supposed to eat right away after they've taken their insulin shots. "I'm all right," I say, hoping that I am.

"And you didn't get enough sleep last night. You were still awake when I got in. You know what Mom says about getting enough sleep."

I know, all right. Courtney can stay up as late as she wants to, but I have to go to bed by ten every night.

Unexpectedly, her tone changes. "Come on, Jane. I don't want anything to happen to you. Besides, I promised Mom I'd look after you."

Courtney is hard to figure out. Sometimes she really does act as if she cares about me.

Even so, I want to talk to Lowell when no one else is around. "You go ahead," I tell her. "I'll be there in a minute."

That makes her mad. She can't handle it if I don't appreciate those rare occasions when she shows concern.

"Okay. But don't blame me if anything happens." She flounces off toward the dining room.

Now I feel guilty, as well as nervous. Why doesn't Lowell come?

Other kids come, alone or in groups of two and three. They wave to me, and some even ask me to join them. Scott rushes by, inquiring about Court. I wonder if I should ask him about Lowell but decide not to.

My stomach growls, and I know I could be making a big mistake. As I stand up at last to go eat, I see Lowell walking stiffly in my direction.

"Hi, Lowell," I squawk, sounding strangely like a seagull. "Can I talk to you?"

He doesn't answer, just keeps walking right on past me.

Maybe he didn't understand my birdlike voice. Maybe he didn't recognize me in this dark lobby. I start after him. "Lowell?"

He turns with a scowl. "Leave me alone." Then he goes to a desk in the lobby and sits down to write.

Even though I know I've got to eat, I feel as if I'm going to throw up.

LOWELL
Wednesday, August 7, 7:25 a.m.
Hotel, Newbury

28

Dear Dad,
Scott just told me about it. Eighty-seven pieces of mail were waiting for our tour at the hotel here in Newbury. Not counting Dr. and Mrs. Phillips, that averages 2.175 letters per person. I was the only one who didn't get anything. You really care about me, don't you?

So what. It doesn't matter if I never hear from you. Or see you either. I'll never forgive you for what you did. Fooling around all that time. Planning for months how you'd get rid of me in England.

I guess you're rid of everyone now. . . .

Dear Dr. Cline,
I'll never be rid of these headaches. I'm getting one already. Before 8 in the morning. I've never had one before 8 in the morning. . . .

JANE
Wednesday, August 7, 12:10 p.m.
Oxford

29

"The green slime," says Teresa.

"Huh?" I say. We're sitting in a pub in Oxford, practically elbow to elbow with the middle-aged tourists at the next table who speak with American accents.

Teresa indicates my plate with a nod. "Don't say I didn't warn you about ordering cooked vegetables in England. You never know what you're eating when you order cooked vegetables here because everything comes out green slime. Broccoli. Brussels sprouts. Dandelion greens. It's all the same."

I take a forkful of something that looks like seaweed and, because eating like a cannibal seems like a good way to punish Lowell Stevens (even though he isn't here to see me), talk with a full mouth. "I need the vitamins."

"Vitamins!" scoffs Teresa, waving the pickle from her Ploughman's Lunch so close I can smell it. Her purple nail polish is chipped, and I notice for the first time that her fingernails have been bitten to the quick. "You won't

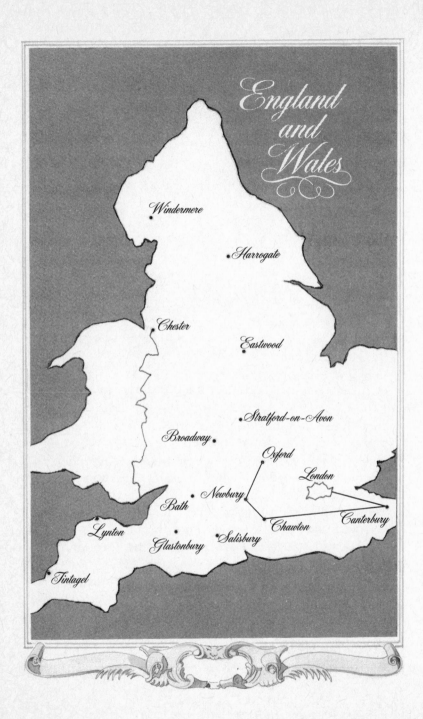

England
and
Wales

Windermere

Harrogate

Chester

Eastwood

Stratford-on-Avon

Broadway

Oxford

London

Newbury

Bath

Chawton

Canterbury

Lynton

Salisbury

Glastonbury

Tintagel

find any vitamins in that muck. They've been boiled to death, if there ever were any. Do you know you could be eating actually anything at all? Hedgerow leaves. Alfalfa. Grasshoppers, even."

The man from the next table nudges my arm. "We could teach these limeys a thing or two about food, couldn't we, girls?" As he rises to leave, his breath trails along my cheek, leaving its message of beer.

I feel a pain in my stomach, like standing behind a batter and catching his swing right in my middle. It's not Teresa, or even the American tourist, who caused it. Karen Kemper has walked into the pub, tugging at Lowell's arm and leading him to the only vacant table. The one the American couple is just leaving.

I try to make myself invisible by pretending enthusiasm for my vegetable slush, but Karen wants us to know they've arrived.

"Hi, Teresa. Hi, Jane. How's the food?"

"Bizarre," says Teresa.

I look up and wave as politely as I'm able.

"The Ploughman's Lunch is stale, and the Vegetable Plate is warmed-over insects," Teresa continues. "Go somewhere else while you still have your health."

Karen ignores this advice. She sits down and picks up a dirty menu. Lowell follows suit, avoiding eye contact with me.

I knew Karen and Lowell were buddies today. I knew they'd been riding together on the bus. But sitting right next to us like this is more than I'm prepared for.

The only defense I can think of is gaiety. "This isn't grasshopper," I tell Teresa in a voice that sounds like fingernails scraping on a chalkboard. "It tastes more like alligator."

Large purple earrings bobble on her ears as Teresa shakes her head. "No way. Alligator meat is too expensive. They only put things like grasshoppers and dandelion greens in green slime because no one can tell the difference anyway. Don't tell me about green slime. I'm an expert on green slime. I live at Old Hen's boarding school, remember."

I take another forkful of whatever it is I'm eating, forcing it down with a gulp of lukewarm water.

From the corner of my eye, I see what's going on at the next table. Karen setting down her beer-stained menu. "Good thing I'm not very hungry." She leans intimately toward Lowell. "Want to share a pastie with me?"

Share a pastie? A pastie, which is a cold meat pie, is practically the same dimensions as McDonald's famous dessert. I picture them passing it back and forth, taking mouse-sized nibbles. Or holding the two ends in their separate mouths and chewing toward the middle.

Lowell doesn't answer, and for one brief self-centered moment, I suspect Karen was delivering that line for my benefit.

Self-centered is right, Jane Johnson! Just because Lowell Stevens was friendly to you for one day—just because he gave you some books and stopped scowling for exactly six hours of the eight days we've been on this tour—doesn't mean you've staked a claim. Grow up. Pack your bags. Shove off.

My fork clangs to the plate with unnecessary noise. "You're right," I tell Teresa. "This stuff is awful. Let's go walk around the university before our bus leaves."

Teresa grabs the check and stands up. "I'm ready."

Ordinarily Teresa is famous for complaining about the walking we have to do. As far as I can tell, she brought mostly high heels with her (at least four pairs plus some drugstore thongs; no Nikes or Adidas like the shoes the rest of us wear), and she limps a lot. But walking through Oxford is a different matter from walking through cathedrals and ruins. Oxford is full of students.

We pay the bill and cross the street toward the old stone buildings, Teresa towering over me in her purple sandals and limping slightly. It's cold outside, and I'm glad I'm wearing jeans, not designer shorts like Teresa's. I study her bare legs for goose bumps and see that they're there, all right. Living with Courtney and Mom, I'm used to people who spend a lot of time worrying about the clothes they wear. But Teresa's the first person I've ever met who doesn't try to be a little bit comfortable now and then.

I realize I shouldn't be staring at someone's legs and look up, at the interesting architecture. Gargoyles on some of the buildings. An ancient bridge spanning one of the streets. Someone once told me that Oxford is the most beautiful university in the world, but on this particular cloud-covered day the yellow stone looks drab. Jaundiced. Or maybe I'm the one who's jaundiced today. I figure I'm entitled.

Even though Oxford is famous for students, Teresa can't see any to talk to. She suggests we follow some tourists who are going inside a building. A man sitting at a desk inside the door tells us we're in the Bodleian Library and that we may want to look at the exhibits in the next room. They turn out to be very old manuscripts, dating back to Celtic (whatever that means) times. I lift the protective canvases one by one, pretending enormous interest.

The truth is that my mind is elsewhere. How could Lowell give me three books yesterday and tell me to leave him alone today? Was it something I did? Was it that silly postcard from Brenda? Or did he just simply lead me on for a while, deliberately being cruel?

Teresa tires quickly of old manuscripts she can't read. "Do you want to know something? This is a drag. Let's go outside. There must be some students somewhere around this university, even if it is summer."

I stay by her side as she limps through a courtyard and back along the sidewalk. Wherever the students are, she can't find them. She is stuck with talking to Plain Jane Johnson, your basic American reject.

"Don't think that Karen's going to win," she tells me.

"Win what?"

"Our contest. You can join if you want to. Don't worry. Karen isn't going to win." Teresa pushes her glasses back up on her nose.

"What contest?"

"To get a boy to ask us to be his buddy. Everyone who wants to join puts twenty-five pounds in the kitty. And the first one who's asked gets it all. There are only eight guys on this tour and thirty-two girls, so it won't be easy for any of us. But we're all fighting the same odds."

"All the girls on the tour have joined?" I ask.

"Of course not. Everyone isn't *invited* to join. Just you and Karen and Glenna Feinstein and me. Just the push-ees."

I don't know Glenna Feinstein very well. She's this tiny brunette from Michigan with an entire wardrobe of jogging suits. She's always bouncing around in a circle or doing warmup exercises while Old Hen is talking. But it occurs to me that Karen and Teresa are certainly not pushees. It occurs to me that Teresa has chosen that word because she can't bring herself to say any of the words that really do apply. Misfits. Oddballs. Yo-yos.

"Don't think that we're going to let people like your sister Courtney horn in," Teresa continues. "No, this is by invitation only. Well, do you want to?"

"I don't know. I can't really afford twenty-five pounds."

"Make up your mind. We're not going to beg you."

"I'd better not," I say. "Thanks anyway."

Teresa stands up straight. In those high heels she's nearly six feet tall. "Just as well," she says. "You wouldn't stand a chance."

"Someone's missing," says Dr. Phillips.

We've just eaten dinner and have gathered in the tiny lobby of the hotel in Stratford before walking to the Royal Shakespeare Theatre for a performance of *King Lear*.

We're all so dressed up I hardly recognize us. I've never seen Dr. Phillips without a coat and tie, but tonight he's wearing a navy blue suit and white shirt. Sylvia, standing by his side, has on a print dress we haven't seen before, and her hair is teased so tight it looks bulletproof. Even Teresa has put aside her shorts for the evening and has managed to find a backless dress to wear with the inevitable high heels and earrings.

Despite the blue suit and his crisp-looking tie, Old Hen looks tense. "Who's missing? Speak up, friends. Who's missing a buddy?"

Karen waves her arm in the air. "I am. Lowell." It's hard to read the expression on her face. Disappointment? Anxiety? Relief?

"Lowell?" says Dr. Phillips. He can't quite digest this piece of information. Mr. Stone Face may keep his sense of humor buried, but he's always *there*, listening in his strange way to Dr. Phillips's lectures. It's unthinkable that Lowell Stevens, of all people, would be late for a chance to see a production of *King Lear* by the Royal Shakespeare Company, right here in Stratford.

Old Hen wipes his forehead with his handkerchief. It's been a bad day. A hundred miles out of Newbury this morning Marjean Axelson remembered she'd left a five-hundred-dollar camera in her room, and we had to go back for it. Merrill Bickerstaff and Ryan Donovan were forty-five minutes late for the bus out of Oxford, and we

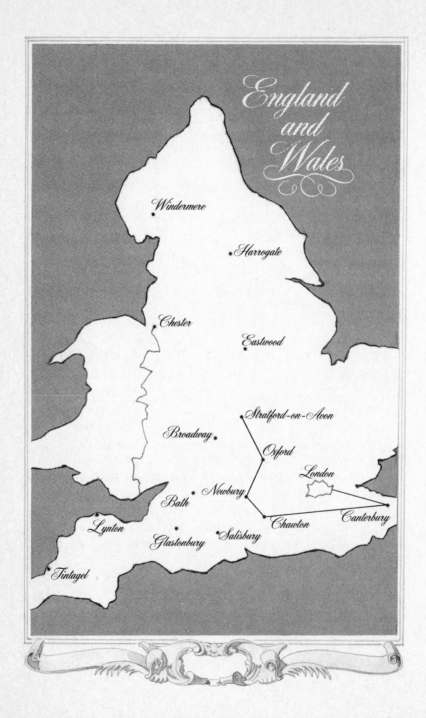

England and Wales

Windermere

Harrogate

Chester

Eastwood

Stratford-on-Avon

Oxford

Broadway

London

Newbury

Bath

Chawton

Canterbury

Lynton

Salisbury

Glastonbury

Tintagel

had to pass up a side trip on our way to Stratford. Old Hen looks tired. He looks, in fact—with his round face and stubby little arms—like an abused Cabbage Patch Doll. I wonder if he's always looked like that or if I've just never paid attention before.

"Where is Lowell?" Old Hen asks Karen.

Now the expression on her face is obvious. Anger. "I don't know!"

Old Hen seems a little angry himself. "This is why we have the buddy system, friends. To keep track of each other."

"He went to his room as soon as we got here. I haven't seen him since," Karen explains. She's not coping with the rebuke. Anger may dissolve to tears.

Old Hen realizes he's touched a nerve and focuses his exasperation elsewhere. "Where's Lowell's roommate? Scott?" he calls out.

Across the room Scott is performing a two-fingered rhythm solo on Courtney's back. He's missed the whole discussion.

"SCOTT!"

Scott interrupts his concert. "Yeah?"

"Do you know where Lowell is?"

"Yeah. Didn't I tell you? He's crashed already."

"Crashed?" repeats Dr. Phillips.

Scott misreads Old Hen's bewilderment for stupidity. "Gone to bed," he translates. "He didn't feel well. Asked me to tell you."

Old Hen exhales slowly, deciding what to say. He decides to let Lowell's defection pass. "All right, friends, we'll walk to the theater together, and I'll give you your tickets there. Don't let your buddies out of your sight. If the two of you get separated from the group, just ask someone how to get to the Royal Shakespeare Theatre. It isn't far. Any questions?"

Karen raises her hand. "I don't have a buddy," she whines.

"Yes, yes," Old Hen mumbles huskily and clears his throat. "Well, you just stick with Lucy Beth—er, Teresa—and her buddy for the time being." Until they get back to Carrington Academy, he has agreed to call Teresa by the name she prefers, but he has a hard time remembering. "All right, friends, follow me."

With Sylvia beside him, he marches to the door in that determined way of his, leaning forward, his hands flapping at his sides like rubber paddles. Always the gentleman, he opens the door for his wife, then hands it off to the next person in the procession.

By the time Teresa and I collect Karen, we are among the last to leave. In the nearly empty lobby I notice something which isn't your basic hotel decor. At least not in the summer. A miniature Christmas tree on a small table is dazzling its corner of the room with colored lights. A sign nearby urges us to make our reservations now for the hotel's holiday parties.

The whole city seems out of synch. We have to sign up on August 7 for our Christmas parties. And Lowell Stevens—the only kid on this tour who has a thimbleful of knowledge about William Shakespeare—is upstairs boycotting the first of our only two chances to see a real live Shakespearean production in Stratford-on-Avon.

As we walk out the door the wind whips my face. I struggle into my raincoat, wishing for the hundredth time that I'd bought the "old lady" blue one in Nordstrom's that had an inner lining instead of the "with it" tan one that Courtney said looked "absolutely fantastic" on me. Teresa doesn't bother to put on the sweater she's carrying, even though the goose bumps on her back are bigger than the ones she had on her legs earlier today.

"Where's Scott?" Karen asks.

Teresa doesn't answer. She's blowing a balloon-sized bubble and has to maintain concentration.

"I've got to talk to Scott," Karen says. "Hurry up." She grabs Teresa by the arm and drags her off the curb and into the street, making an end run around the other members of the tour in front of us. I follow dutifully. A dazed quarterback using any kind of interference.

When we reach Scott and Courtney, Karen releases her hold on Teresa's arm and seizes Scott's instead. "What's the matter with Lowell?"

"You haven't noticed?" Scott asks.

"Noticed what?" says Karen.

"He's out of tune."

Karen doesn't understand Scott's rock star lingo. "What?"

"He's gone. Disappeared. He's never been here. He's the worst roommate I could have been stuck with."

Karen is still confused. "How sick is he?"

"Straitjacket case for sure. What a loser. Can't take any razzing at all."

Court is suddenly interested. "What happened?"

"Oh, he got a postcard, for a change," says Scott. "Picture of a hotel in Bermuda. First piece of mail he's had. He was the only kid who didn't get any mail in Newbury."

I've already had the feeling that Scott takes too much interest in other people's mail.

"So?" says Teresa.

"Well, I rode him about it, more or less, seeing he hasn't had anything before. Holy Moses, it was just a joke. All I said was, 'So this is why you haven't had any mail before. Your Dad's been banging around Bermuda again with some chick.' Then Lowell starts yelling at me. 'What do you mean *again?*' he says and tries to grab the card out of my hands. But I'm still hanging onto it, and I say, 'Well, it sounds like those two have been to Bermuda together before because your dad says they've decided the ocean looks bluer this time.' Then Lowell goes crazy. He pushes me and hits me trying to get the card away from me, so I have to protect myself, more or less. The stupid card tears while we're fighting and Lowell gets even more upset because he can't read it. When he finally puts it together and figures out what it is his dad has to say, he picks up a chair and throws it across the room. So I decide I've had enough of his temper tantrums and come downstairs to the lobby."

I try to picture Lowell engaged in violence like hitting Scott and throwing chairs across the room. It doesn't focus. The Lowell I know just scowls at people or looks away when he's mad.

"He isn't really sick then," says Karen. She's assuring herself, not the rest of us. "I'm going to go back and get him."

"I wouldn't if I were you," Scott says. "I tried going back a little while later, hoping he'd cooled down. He was lying on his bed, crying. A sixteen-year-old kid bawling his eyes out over a stupid postcard from his dad. When I told him to put his act together and get dressed for the play, he said he didn't feel like it. He said to tell Old Hen he was sick."

An idea suddenly hits me. All that time I thought Lowell was on drugs because his eyes were red. Maybe he wasn't stoned, maybe he'd been crying. Or just wasn't able to sleep.

LOWELL
Wednesday, August 7, 10:20 p.m.
Hotel, Stratford

31

Dear Dad,
Here's something for you from George Bernard Shaw and me: If you strike a child, strike it in anger. A blow in cold blood neither can nor should be forgiven. . . .

Dear Chris,
You'll be sorry you got pregnant. I've always known you were stupid. . . .

LOWELL
Thursday, August 8, 7:45 a.m.
Hotel, Stratford
32

Dear Dr. Cline,

You're right. Crying really does help. Last night was so bad I was sure I was going crazy (I've suspected it for a long time). I've never cried so hard, not even when I was a little kid. But afterwards I went to sleep for eight hours, and this morning I feel better than I have in weeks. Physically, that is.

Mentally I'm a little better, too. I'm not even so mad at Jill for getting leukemia and dying.

Now if I can just work up the courage to apologize to someone, maybe I'll even like myself. . . .

JANE
Thursday, August 8, 9:35 a.m.
Stratford
33

Glenna Feinstein and I end up being buddies today. I can't exactly recall either one of us inviting the other, but we seemed to be the leftovers after everyone else paired off at breakfast. Maybe Glenna's a pushee, after all.

Today's an important day for buddies. Stratford is the first city since London where we'll stay more than one night in the same hotel. And it's the only place so far where we'll be on our own most of the day. Dr. Phillips has given us maps to the town and explained how to walk to "historical sites" like Shakespeare's birthplace and the church where he was buried. We're free until 4:00 p.m. when the bus picks us up at the hotel and drives us to Anne Hathaway's cottage, just outside town.

Right now we're on our way to an even more important site than Shakespeare's birthplace. A laundromat. Glenna found the address in the phone book and figured out on the map how to walk there.

Boy, do I need a laundromat. After scrubbing my clothes in hotel washbasins for a week, my underwear looks as gray as a British sky.

The buildings we pass are terrific. Most of them are very old and are built in the half-timbered style that sixteenth-century England was famous for. Wood framing on the outside. Spaces filled with masonry. The windows are normal size but made up of dozens of tiny panes.

I'm grateful for the unusual architecture because it gives me something to exclaim about. An excuse to stop and rest now and then. This plastic bag full of dirty jeans and other laundry is heavy and awkward. I set it on the sidewalk, panting.

"Here, I'll carry that for you," Glenna says.

Glenna Feinstein is the only person I've ever met who makes me feel like the Incredible Hulk. I'm not quite five feet three in my bare feet, but I obliterate her. She can't be more than four feet ten.

"You're already carrying a bag," I protest. I have a sneaking suspicion, in fact, that her laundry bag may be heavier than mine.

She whisks up my bag from the sidewalk and settles it on her free shoulder, as if it were an empty knapsack. "No problem," she says. "I have to do harder things than this when I'm in training."

We fall into step again along the Stratford streets. "What are you in training for?" I ask.

"Well, I'm not in training *now*," she says. "My parents made me come to Europe to get away from gymnastics for awhile. They think I'm getting too one-sided."

I try to remember Teresa's definition of pushers and pushees. What was it she said? *All of us are here either because we pushed our parents to send us to Europe or they pushed us to come*. I realize that in the week since Teresa told me that, I've sort of made up my own definition. Both pushers and pushees are kids who haven't mastered the art of getting along with other kids.

By Teresa's definition Glenna is a pushee. By mine the jury is still out.

"Why didn't you want to come to Europe?" I ask.

"You kidding? I can't afford to lose three weeks of training. Not if I'm going to be a medalist at the next Olympics. I cried for two days when my parents told me I had to come on this trip. I've given up everything for gymnastics. Parties. Movies. Football games. Dates. I'm probably the only fourteen-year-old you've ever met who's never had a date."

"Wrong," I say. "There are two of us. Three, really. My best friend, Brenda, back home, is another."

"There are more than that," says Glenna. "All the girls I work out with put gymnastics training first. They don't do anything else either. That's why I can't afford to be over here in England wasting time."

Dumbfounded, I stop walking. "Wasting time? You're not wasting time."

She stops walking, too, and puts the bags down on the sidewalk. "Yes, I am. I'm not training, and I'm not having any fun either. I don't know how to talk to anyone but gymnasts. This tour has been a drag."

For a minute I almost start reciting Mom's Lesson Number One but regain my sanity in time. Get that. Jane Johnson almost telling someone how to be an extrovert. Instead I pick up my bag. "I'm rested now. Thanks for carrying this for me."

Glenna picks up her own bag and we start walking again. "It paralyzes me to talk to guys," she continues, "but I can't even make sense when I talk to girls I don't know very well. Teresa asked me to join a contest that costs twenty-five pounds. The first girl who's asked by a boy to be his buddy wins the pot. I don't have twenty-five pounds to lose, and I know I'll never win. But I didn't know how to tell Teresa that I didn't want to enter."

"I'll tell her for you," I offer.

"It's too late. I've already given her my money. It wouldn't be sportsmanlike to ask for it back now."

Sportsmanlike. A gymnast's word. Not universally understood.

We reach the laundromat and I hold the door open for Glenna, wondering how I can help with her more important problems.

All at once my legs turn to whipped cream. Ryan and Lowell are inside, stuffing dirty socks and T-shirts into machines.

I actually turn part way around, preparing to bolt. Then I realize what a stinking trick that would be to play on Glenna, so I throw back my shoulders and try to look nonchalant—which will be hard to do under the circumstances. The only free washing machines are right next to the ones the guys are using.

Stay with me, Glenna, I'm thinking. We've got to stay together.

I follow her to the wall, where she's trying to get soap from a machine.

Ryan looks up from a pair of scrungy shorts and gives me a half-salute.

I wave back.

"Hi," says Lowell.

"Hi," I say, trying to strike the perfect balance between civility and aloofness. I need gymnastics training.

Planting himself in my path, Lowell puts his thumbs in the pockets of his jeans and looks straight through me. "Have you been avoiding me or something?"

Now I'm really nervous. How do you deal with a guy who insults you one day and pretends to flirt with you the next? Is he just setting me up so he can do something horrible to me tomorrow? "Uh—" I begin.

Glenna rescues me from fifteen feet away. "Do you have any ten-pence pieces?" she calls.

Lowell doesn't budge. I have to walk around him to reach Glenna. "Just three," I say, handing them over to her.

Her mouth twists into a frown as she studies the coins in her hand. "That won't be enough for one load apiece." She turns to Lowell who has shadowed me across the room. "Do you have any ten-pence pieces?"

"No," he says without checking.

"Go ask Ryan," she tells me.

"He doesn't have any either," Lowell says.

Glenna sighs. "Well, I'll go find change somewhere."

"I'll go," I offer quickly.

"Yes, Jane and I will go," Lowell tells Glenna. "You stay here and keep Ryan company." He takes me by the elbow and leads me briskly toward the door. My elbow feels like hot coals. Everywhere else I'm icicles.

Outside the sky has turned blue. A nice day, after all.

Lowell squeezes my arm. "That was a generous thing we just did."

"Huh?" My mind's in slow motion.

"Leaving Ryan and Glenna alone. They're crazy about each other."

That couldn't be right. Glenna's too interested in gymnastics to notice boys. "Are you sure?"

"Would I lie about something that important? Of course, they may not know it yet." He smiles at his stupid joke, showing those big white teeth. Whiter than the clouds that have appeared. Brighter than the sun.

I can't help myself. I smile, too.

"That's better," he says. "For thirty-six hours I've been afraid you were going to deck me. Not that I don't deserve it. I was rotten to you yesterday morning."

"No, you weren't," I lie.

"But now that I've apologized and you've forgiven

me"—he pauses, waiting to see if I get the new joke any faster—"maybe you'll tell me what was on your mind."

"I—uh—can't remember," I lie again.

"Waiting for a real apology, huh?" Lowell stops walking and lets go of my arm. "Okay, you deserve it." He brushes at a noisy fly, circling about our heads. "I'm sorry, Jane. I've been hating myself worse than you've hated me. It's just that—" He scratches his nose with the back of his fist, hesitating.

"What?" I urge.

"Never mind. I can't talk about it right now. Look, how does a picnic sound? I found a dynamite little spot by the Avon for lunch. As soon as we've finished our laundry, we'll round up the Great American Lovers"—he nods toward the laundromat—"and go visit Shakespeare's birthplace. By then we'll be so worn out that we'll be ready to lie by the river forever. How about it?"

"Sounds like fun."

He smiles.

Lowell Stevens' smile could make orchids bloom.

JANE
Thursday, August 8, 2:45 p.m.
Avon River, Stratford

34

Lowell winks at me. "See, I told you they were crazy about each other."

Ryan and Glenna have gone off a few yards from us to do back flips and rolls. It turns out that a few years ago, before he started growing so fast, Ryan planned to become a gymnast, too.

I take off my shoes and curl my feet up under me. "Yeah, I guess you're not a bad Merlin, after all."

Lowell and I are sitting by the Avon River, on the

plastic drip cloth that Glenna was clever enough to buy at a paint store. We've finished our lunch of cheese sandwiches, milk, and fruit, and are enjoying the chance to relax for a little while—just about the first opportunity we've had to do that on this tour.

"Aren't those swans beautiful?" I say. "I wish we had more bread to feed them."

"You gave them practically your whole sandwich," Lowell reminds me.

This isn't exactly the time to mention that I'm supposed to take it easy on white bread, so I change the subject. "I wonder if Shakespeare used to come here and feed bread to the great, great, great grandparents of these swans," I say.

"Contentment in one's life are these, A flowing river, bread and cheese," Lowell recites.

"William Shakespeare?" I ask.

Lowell grins. "Lowell Vincent Stevens. One of his sappier tenth-grade efforts. But thanks for the compliment."

"I knew it," I exclaim. "I knew you wrote poetry. The first time I looked at you I knew you wrote poetry."

"Is that why you kept staring at me? Because you thought I was some nerd who writes poetry?"

"I like poetry! Recite another one for me."

Lowell picks up a flat rock and skips it along the surface of the river. "My poems aren't worth memorizing. Besides, my English teacher kept us too busy memorizing other people's stuff."

The conversation seems to be dying, and I struggle for some way to keep it alive. "I take it you've already been in the tenth grade. Will you be a junior in the fall?"

Making a pillow of his clasped hands, Lowell lies down on the plastic and studies the limb of a nearby tree. "Senior."

"Gee, I didn't realize you were that old."

"I guess that depends on what you consider old," he says.

"Well, seniors seem old to me. I'll just be a freshman when school starts. Ninth grade."

"Yeah, Scott told me. I even know how old you are. Fourteen last February." He rolls over and rests on an elbow so he can face me. "How old do you think I am?"

That's hard to figure out. Lowell doesn't look any older than Scott, but he seems more grown up, somehow. "Seventeen," I say. "Maybe eighteen."

"I was sixteen last month," Lowell tells me. "I'm not quite a year and a half older than you are."

"Sixteen! And you'll be a senior this fall?"

Lowell shrugs. "So I skipped a couple of grades. No big deal."

"No wonder you always know so much. You're a senior who's skipped two grades."

"Look, I said it's no big deal. Guys like Merrill and Ryan are jocks. Scott's into music and dancing. My specialty is books, I guess."

"Of course it's a big deal," I say. "I'd love to be as smart and worldly as you are."

Lowell rolls on his stomach and rests his chin on both hands. "I'll tell you something. Being smart isn't all that wonderful. Everyone treats you like a freak. Your dad thinks that anyone over five feet eleven should be into the macho football routine, so he worries that you may be missing a few hormones. Your English teacher thinks you're too young to read the dirty passages in the Mailer and Updike books that he's assigned to the other kids in the class. And freshman girls, who aren't even a year and a half younger than you are, think you're too worldly for them."

"I didn't say that," I tell him.

"Good. Then you'll do it," he says.

"Do what?" I ask.

"Be my buddy tomorrow."

Did I hear him right? Did he really ask me to be his buddy?

"Well?" he says, sitting up.

Yes, he did ask me. So there, Teresa! Too bad I didn't enter your stupid pot.

"Sure," I say, "I'd like that."

He shakes his head, as if this conversation isn't going the way he planned.

"What's the matter?" I ask.

"Sometimes I can't believe you're real," he tells me. "There's absolutely no guile in you, is there, Jane? You're completely ingenuous."

I don't understand exactly what he's saying. I'm not positive what those words mean.

"Any other girl, if I'd treated her the way I treated you yesterday, would make me suffer for a while before she gave in. But you just look at me and smile. The same way you forgave me when I apologized this morning outside the laundromat."

I play with the hem of my cardigan. "I guess I don't know much about boys. I've never been on a date."

"See, there you go again," he tells me. "Never having had a date isn't something that your normal girl admits to a guy. Normal girls always want guys to think that they've been around."

I bite my lip, still looking down at my sweater. "I'm sorry you think I'm abnormal."

He takes my chin and lifts it up so we're looking eye-to-eye. "Hey, I don't think you're abnormal. I think you're supernormal."

Embarrassed, I try to pull away, but his hand grips me tighter.

"Shall I tell you what else I think about you?" he asks.

His eyes are like two bullets, ready to fire. I wish he'd let go of my chin so I didn't have to look at them. "I guess so," I say.

"I think you have it all over Eleanor of Aquitaine," Lowell tells me. "She was full of guile. Besides, I bet she didn't have dimples."

I can't help myself. I grin.

"There they are," Lowell says. "I guess I could teach that old Merlin a trick or two."

JANE
Thursday, August 8, 10:25 p.m.
Stratford

35

Court rolls her eyes at the ceiling when she sees Lowell and me holding hands in the lobby of the Royal Shakespeare Theatre. The truth is that we've been holding hands for two hours—all during the performance of *The Taming of the Shrew*. Lowell traded seats with Glenna, just so he could sit next to me.

Suddenly a perfectly innocent expression of affection seems dirty, and I try to let go. But Lowell, who doesn't have to live with my big sister and isn't intimidated by her, squeezes my hand tighter so I can't.

Sensing defiance, Court barks orders like a drill sergeant. "Go straight back to the hotel, Jane. It's after your bedtime."

Oh, brother. Talk about being treated like your basic kindergartner.

Lowell just grins at her. "Sure, Courtney, I'll have her back right away. Before you even turn into a pumpkin."

"I'll count on that," Courtney replies tartly. She grabs Scott's arm and they head toward the door.

I don't know what to say. Should I thank Lowell for sticking up for me, or what? While I'm trying to decide, Glenna and Ryan walk up.

"Why don't we walk back by way of that ice cream store we saw?" Ryan suggests. "Maybe it's still open."

I'm not thrilled about that idea. Ice cream isn't something Dr. Lieberman likes me to eat. And watching other people enjoy themselves sounds like a boring way to get me into more trouble with Court.

"You two decide," Glenna says to the guys. "Jane and I are going to make a trip to the water closet."

How did she know I'm ready to burst?

But when we get to the ladies' room, Glenna has something else in mind. She throws her arms around me. "I did it! I won Teresa's pot! Seventy-five pounds! Ryan asked me to be his buddy tomorrow."

"Hey, that's great," I tell her. "Are you and Ryan becoming an item or something?"

"Heck no. I don't have time for guys. At least I won't after this trip is over."

"But you two really seemed to hit it off today."

Glenna shrugs. "I guess so. He's a lot of fun. But I don't want to get involved with anyone. That would just make things harder for me when I go home and start concentrating on gymnastics again."

For no reason that news depresses me. Why should I care if Glenna isn't in the market for a summer romance?

"Anyway, I wanted to thank you for helping me. I never would have won that money without your help," Glenna tells me.

"I didn't help you," I say.

"Sure, you did. If I hadn't been your buddy today and tagged along with you and Lowell, it never would have happened. Well, let's go back and find the guys."

"I'll be there in a minute," I tell her. "I really do need to use this bathroom."

When I return, the lobby seems strangely silent and prematurely dimmed. Lowell is standing alone, studying some posters of the Shakespearean players.

"Where are Glenna and Ryan?" I ask him.

"I told them I didn't feel like ice cream tonight. You don't mind, do you? I've noticed you never eat it." He studies me with narrowed eyes, a tenseness on his face.

"No," I say, and Lowell sighs, his brow softening.

But I wonder how I really do feel. Am I glad that he's paid that much attention to me or nervous that he's figured out I have diabetes? Or am I simply pleased to have a few more moments with him alone on this moon-cheered night?

Lowell helps me into my coat and then fastens the buttons of his leather jacket, all six of them through the six holes. "Who sewed your button on for you?" I say, disappointed that he didn't ask me to do it. Maybe I should have volunteered.

"I did, of course. You think I'm helpless or something?"

"Well, my father couldn't do it," I explain as the first blast of outdoor air punishes my face. "He wouldn't even know how to thread the needle."

"My father wouldn't either, but those old-fashioned guys are more to be pitied than censured. Some of the best times I have are whipping up masterpieces in the kitchen. You ought to taste my curried crab divan."

We're down the steps now, walking, and I suddenly feel panicky and disoriented even though Lowell is holding me securely on my arm. "Isn't the hotel over that way?" I ask.

"Yep."

"Well, where are we going?"

"You'll see."

He's right, of course. I do see in a few minutes. He's led me to the river where the moon glows iridescently on its surface.

"We couldn't leave Stratford tomorrow without saying good-bye to the great great great grandchildren of Shakespeare's swans, could we?" Lowell asks.

Okay, I can go along with his silly joke. But I giggle, feeling like a little kid. "Good-bye, swans," I say.

Lowell says nothing but holds me by both hands, drawing me so close I smell the rich, masculine odor of his leather jacket. Belatedly I realize he doesn't have swans on his mind but something more important, something more personal. If I didn't know he had a girlfriend back home—if I didn't know he respected people who were "faithful"—if I didn't know he was older than I am and much more worldly—I'd think he was trying to work up the courage to kiss me. I shiver, waiting to find out for sure.

I don't even hear the footsteps of people approaching from behind. "Well, look who's here," says Scott.

"I thought you two were going straight to the hotel," Courtney accuses.

"I said I'd get her back before you turned into a pumpkin," Lowell replies. "See, you haven't done it yet."

Courtney, who isn't amused, turns her attention to me. "Scott and I will walk you back to the hotel." She takes me firmly by the arm.

"Oh, Court-ney!"

Lowell takes me by the other arm. "I'll see she gets back safely, Court." His face looks unreal, masklike in the moonlight.

"You better come with me, Jane, if you know what's good for you."

I hesitate, wondering what threat Courtney has in mind. Is she going to tell Lowell about my diabetes? "Why don't we all walk back together?" I ask him.

"Because I'm not ready to go back, and I don't think you are either."

"I—I think I'd better."

He lets go of my arm with a shove. "Go on then. *Go on!*" Stuffing his hands into his pockets, he scuffles off alone toward the river.

LOWELL
Friday, August 9, 1:30 a.m.
Hotel, Stratford

36

Dear Dr. Cline,
    My head is killing me again. Maybe I really am going crazy. All those months while Jill was sick I could handle anything. For her sake I always acted cheerful, even when I wasn't. But now the least little problem sets me off. Today things were going great. I felt like a normal kid for a change. Then something made me mad, and I couldn't control myself any longer. I knew I was overreacting, but I just kept acting like a jackass anyway. And suddenly I felt a grenade exploding inside my skull. . . .

JANE
Friday, August 9, 6:30 a.m.
Hotel, Stratford

37

A fly lands on Courtney's forehead, but Sleeping Beauty doesn't stir. Court could sleep through a nuclear war and not wake up until the earth had revegetated itself. Good thing I'm the one who has to take shots on schedule. She'd be dead by now.

I get out the glucometer and give myself the old sugar test. Darn. Now for the really bad part. Oof. My eyes water as I withdraw the needle from my stomach and press some cotton to the spot.

I change outfits three times before settling on my blue wrap-around skirt and plaid blouse. I've got to look my best for my day as Lowell's buddy.

Please, Lowell. Please don't still be mad at me about last night.

Have I remembered everything I'll need in my carry-on? Reading matter—just in case. Notebooks. (I've jotted down some ideas and sketches for the tour scrapbook, which I want to show Lowell.)

Please talk to me, Lowell.

Camera.

Don't you think we should take more pictures of Stratford in the early light this morning? Shouldn't we take more pictures of the swans?

Oranges and cheese left over from yesterday's picnic in case the hotel isn't serving breakfast this early.

Everything else goes into my big suitcase, which I put outside the door for the porter to pick up.

There. That seems to be everything.

I sling the carry-on over my shoulder, quietly shut the door so I won't disturb Court, and check my watch again. 6:45. Exactly the time we agreed on.

Taking a deep breath, I walk down the rickety, uneven corridor of this old, old hotel to meet—whom? Dr. Jekyll? Or Mr. Hyde?

Oh please, Lowell. Try to understand about last night. Please don't treat me the way you did that first week in London.

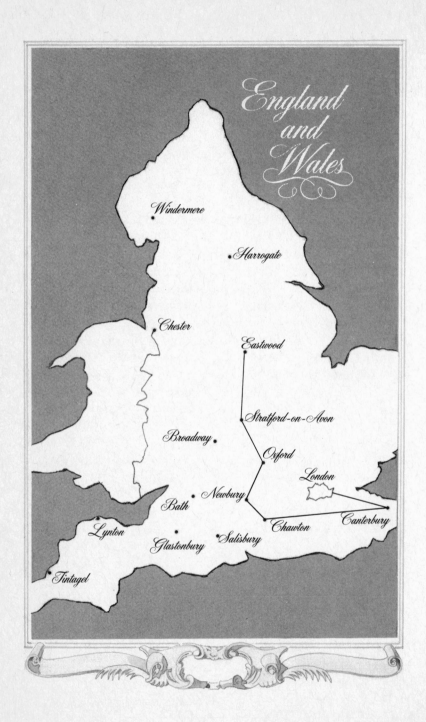

England
and
Wales

Windermere

Harrogate

Chester

Eastwood

Stratford-on-Avon

Broadway

Oxford

London

Newbury

Bath

Chawton

Canterbury

Lynton

Glastonbury

Salisbury

Tintagel

"When I was your age, friends, our public librarian considered the works of D. H. Lawrence obscene. She kept them in a locked case that people under twenty-one weren't allowed access to. Even adults couldn't check them out overnight."

If it was Old Hen's purpose to stir up interest in D. H. Lawrence, he surely succeeded. Some of the kids, who are sick of authors after two nights of Shakespearean plays and a really gosh-awful performance of Agatha Christie last night in Nottingham, have been grumbling about stopping to see Lawrence's birthplace in Eastwood, about five miles out of the city.

Lowell, who's interested in my ideas for the scrapbook and wants to use some of them for his literary magazine, has treated me with reserve all morning.

We thread our way through parked cars and tourists walking in the opposite direction. Past the window of a craft shop where a potter in a leather apron smooths his clay with square thumbs. Along the rain-soaked alley, turned gray to match the sky. Around the corner where a plaque above the emerald door tells us number 8a Victoria Street is the birthplace of D. H. Lawrence.

Despite the lace tablecloth, the plants, the framed pictures—the parlor seems dingy. And small. So small we can't all fit inside. Through the open door our group swirls out on the sidewalk. A kite tail in the wind.

A frumpy, gray-haired lady welcomes us with a Cookie Monster smile. "Crowd in. Crowd in. There's room for everyone if we'll all just—" She misses a beat in her greeting as something catches her attention. "—Hold our breath," she finishes lamely.

I turn to my right to see what threw off her timing. Sylvia is clutching Merrill's arm as if it were a solid-gold baseball bat.

To those of us who know Sylvia, that scene isn't your basic shocker. She's just a friendly lady who tries to compensate for her husband's formality by befriending all of us in turn. But I do remember how she upset me (yes, I can admit it now) when she hung onto Lowell at Hampton Court. So I try to imagine how Sylvia and Merrill must appear to our guide: An overdevoted mother hanging onto her favorite son? A rich old widow with her fortune-hunting suitor? A pathetic dowager with her hired escort? The possibilities almost boggle the mind.

Our guide can't look at the Odd Couple. Her eyes rest elsewhere. On a pale landscape hanging high above our heads, almost to the ceiling. On two porcelain dogs on the mantelpiece. On the handkerchief she twists in red palms. Still her smile doesn't return.

She speaks in well-rehearsed sentences. David Herbert Lawrence was born in this home on September 11, 1885, the fourth child of Arthur and Lydia Lawrence. The house was owned by the coal mining company for which the senior Lawrence worked and was rented to him for two shillings a week, less than fifty cents.

I picture Arthur Lawrence returning to this bathless home after wearying hours below ground, spreading the soot and the gloom of the coal mine over everything inside.

Only two rooms on the first floor. The tiny parlor and a still smaller kitchen. We pass through them on the way to steep, dark stairs that lead to the parents' bedroom. Then to another room (added since the Lawrences moved) where our guide continues her speech.

D. H. Lawrence (or Bert, as his family called him) was his mother's pet among all five children. Believing him to have great talent, she praised, coddled, and catered to him. As a result he was never able to establish a lasting relationship with women his own age but eloped with an older woman (sister of the famous Red Baron of Germany) while she was still married to Lawrence's professor.

Still clinging to Merrill, Sylvia has claimed a spot not two feet from the guide, who is so unnerved by their presence that she can't look at any of us but twists her handkerchief into a damp cord.

Poor Sylvia has no idea what's going on. And Merrill, as usual, probably hasn't even been listening.

I look toward Lowell to send him this private message with a wink but find that he has withdrawn from the group and is standing just beyond the door in the senior Lawrences' bedroom. For some reason he seems troubled, too, as he grinds the sole of his Puma on the bare wooden floor.

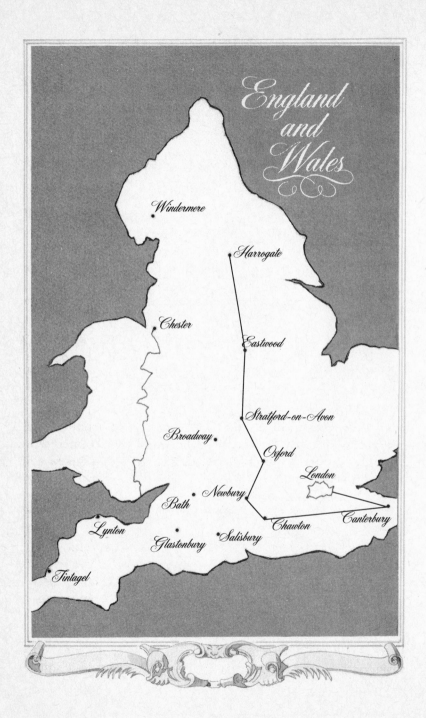

England
and
Wales

Windermere

Harrogate

Chester

Eastwood

Stratford-on-Avon

Broadway

Oxford

London

Newbury

Bath

Canterbury

Lynton

Chawton

Glastonbury • Salisbury

Tintagel

LOWELL
Saturday, August 10, 4:40 p.m.
Hotel, Harrogate

39

Dear Mom,
  I'm not going to call you Jill anymore. It isn't natural. . . .

Dear Mr. Stringham,
  This girl I've met on the tour has given me some great new
ideas for the literary magazine. Layout. Graphics. Table of con-
tents. I can hardly wait to talk to you.

JANE
Saturday, August 10, 7:10 p.m.
Hotel, Harrogate

40

"Hey," Lowell says to me, "do you like Gilbert and Sullivan?"

We're just finishing dessert in the dining room of the hotel in Harrogate. Thick-crusted apple pie topped with whipped cream for the others and a wedge of lukewarm melon for me.

"Yeah," I say expectantly, waiting for him to go on.

But Scott speaks next. "Gilbert and Sullivan? They were okay, I guess."

"I think *Pirates of Penzance* is absolutely fantastic," Courtney chimes in. "Our school put it on last year."

"Do you want to know the very best Gilbert and Sullivan opera?" asks Teresa. "*The Mikado.* I saw it three times last year on television."

No one seems inclined to challenge Teresa's authority, and in the brief silence Lowell turns back to me. "The desk clerk told me there's a concert hall a couple of blocks up the street. They're doing selections from different Gilbert and Sullivan operas. Want to go?"

Do I? He's acting like himself again. The Lowell who kidnapped me from the laundromat in Stratford and took me on a picnic. The Lowell who held my hand all during *The Taming of the Shrew*. The Lowell who walked me back again to the river after dark.

"Let's all go," suggests Teresa. "You want to, don't you, Karen?" It's a statement, not a question.

Karen shrugs. She hasn't been herself since Lowell stood her up that first night in Stratford.

"Yeah, let's all go," Scott echoes.

Lowell frowns at his watch. "We only have twenty minutes. Come on, Jane. We've got to hurry."

Courtney grabs my arm. "Jane can't go. You said you wanted to write to the folks and Brenda tonight. Don't you remember?"

Yes, but that was before Lowell had suggested the concert. Before he started making me feel special again. Right now the thought of spending the evening with him is the most important thing in the world.

"I can write letters any time," I tell her. I turn back to look at Lowell. "I want to go to the concert."

Courtney pauses, then shares her Patty Popular smile with everyone at the table.

"Okay, let's all go get our coats," she says brightly. "Jane and I will meet you in the lobby in a few minutes."

The six of us take off in three different directions, but as soon as we're alone, Court's cheerful tone evaporates. She turns to face me, a hard look showing around her mouth. "Okay, Jane, it's up to you. Either you start going to bed every night before ten o'clock, or I'll tell everyone— and I mean *everyone*—that you have diabetes."

I gasp. "You wouldn't."

"Oh yeah. You just try me."

It's not until after she has left for the concert and I'm in the room alone that a terrible thought hits me. Courtney doesn't really care if I get to bed every night by ten o'clock. What she's trying to do is keep me away from Lowell.

JANE
Saturday, August 10, 4:40 p.m.
Hotel, Harrogate

41

Brenda McConnell
966 Kenton Drive
Atherton, California 94026

Dear Fuzzhead,
Boy, should you be flattered. The gang has gone to a Gilbert and Sullivan concert tonight, but I stayed here in my hotel room so I could write to you. How lucky can one fuzzhead get?
Actually, I just realized that if I don't write to you tonight, I'll beat this letter home. I can't believe that I've been gone 11½ days (more than half of the trip is over!). In some ways it seems that I came to England only yesterday, and in others it seems I've been here all my life. All I know is that I've loved this trip and am going to have withdrawal symptoms when I get home. I wish you and my parents were with me so that I never had to go back.
There's so much to see and absorb that I can't handle it all. Some days go by in a blur, like a movie camera panning too fast. Old Hen (Dr. Phillips to you) keeps us so busy bumping around the highways in a bus or walking through cathedrals and ruins and authors' homes that I can't keep up with my laundry (let alone write letters). Mom's washer and dryer are two things I really miss. Talk about Gray Creep. My underwear has galloping grunge. We head tomorrow for Windermere in the Lake Country, where we'll spend 2 whole nights in the same hotel. That means I may even have time to look for a real laundromat.
About your tacky postcard. It's a good thing a certain person I've met has a sense of humor or you could have gotten me into

real trouble. That's all you deserve to hear about him right now. But if you'll get on your knees and apologize, maybe I'll tell you more (not everything, of course!) about Lowell Stevens when I get home.

See you soon.

Hugs, Jane

Mr. and Mrs. Harden Johnson
975 Kenton Drive
Atherton, California 94026

Dear Dad and Mom,

You can relax. Good old Courtney is doing her duty and taking special care of me. (Too special, if you ask me.) She and some other kids went to a concert tonight, but she made me stay in the hotel so I could go to bed early. Oh well, it gives me a chance to tell you something I haven't been able to say in person lately.

I love you.

I love you.

I love you.

I also love this trip to England and thank you for making it possible. The English countryside looks exactly like the pictures in those old-fashioned storybooks Grandma used to send me. Rolling hills. Quaint hedgerows separating the farms. And everything so green that when I look out the bus window I feel I'm seeing a TV commercial for fertilizer.

The kids on the tour are great, too. I've made such wonderful new friends that I know it will be very hard to leave some of them. If I didn't miss the two of you and Brenda so much, I might never go home.

Well, it won't be long now.

Dear Courtney,
    Why don't you and Scott mind your own business? . . .

Dear Chris,
    It was your own fault you got pregnant, so you'll just have to suffer the consequences. I'm not going to have anything to do with you or the baby either. . . .

Dear Dr. Cline,
    I'm furious, but I didn't do anything stupid for a change. Why? Because of Jane? Because this time I'm sure she wanted to go with me? Because I finally think she likes me? . . .

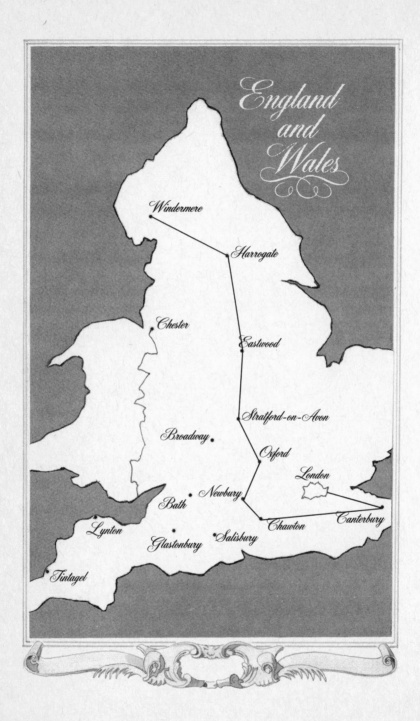

England and Wales

- Windermere
- Harrogate
- Chester
- Eastwood
- Stratford-on-Avon
- Broadway
- Orford
- London
- Newbury
- Bath
- Chawton
- Canterbury
- Lynton
- Glastonbury
- Salisbury
- Tintagel

"I don't think I'll ever enjoy reading Wordsworth's poetry again," I tell Lowell. "Imagine making his sister and children sleep in that ice closet of a room while he keeps the two biggest and warmest rooms in the house for his own bedroom and office."

Lowell doesn't answer, so I continue with my list of grievances against the selfish poet. "And how would you like to be a member of his family and eat porridge two meals a day for every single day of the year? No wonder Sir Walter Scott escaped out the window and went to the local pub for a good meal whenever he was a guest in Wordsworth's house."

Despite the cold, Lowell and I are sitting on a bench outside our hotel in Windermere, discussing the authors whose houses we visited today—John Ruskin, Beatrix Potter, and William Wordsworth. Of all the hotels we've stayed in so far this one certainly has the most beautiful grounds and the most breathtaking view. From the bench where we're sitting we look right down on the tranquil lake and on the dock from which the boats leave. Or at least we could have looked down on those things a few hours ago, before it got dark. Now the outlines of the lake are so indistinct we have to trust our senses of hearing and smell for assurance that Lake Windermere is still there.

Something occurs to me. This isn't a discussion at all. Lowell, who usually has far more to say about poets and literature than I do, is letting me do all the talking.

"Is something the matter?" I ask him.

Without speaking, he grabs me with both arms and our lips meet in a long, gentle kiss. Now I know for sure what he planned to do that night in Stratford and why he was so mad at me and Court.

At last I pull away and bury my face in his leathery-smelling shoulder. "Oh, Lowell."

He holds me tight for awhile, then kisses me again. I'm startled by the urgency—the wetness—of his mouth. But I don't really mind. In fact, I like it so much I lose all sense of time.

JANE
Sunday, August 11, 11:12 p.m.
Hotel, Windermere

44

I can't believe it's so late that Courtney's already in bed. She's there, all right, though, dressed in her nightgown and sitting up with the light on, ready to impale me with her eyes when I walk in the room.

"Do you know what time it is?" she demands. The lamp on the night table is too dim to illuminate this entire high-ceilinged room but fixes a sickly yellow on Courtney's face, sharpening her features and etching weird lines in her forehead.

"Not exactly," I say. "Ten o'clock maybe."

She nods toward the clock on the night table. "It's twelve minutes after eleven."

"I'm sorry. I didn't have my watch on."

"I've been worried sick," she exclaims. "Something could have happened to you. You might have been lying out in the cold in hypoglycemic reaction."

"Oh Court, you haven't been in bed before two o'clock a single night since we've been on this trip. Just because you accidentally get in before I do for once doesn't mean I'm dead or anything. Why are you back so early, anyway?"

"Don't change the subject. I'm not on the witness stand. You are. Sit down," she commands.

"Let me go to the bathroom first. I'm dying." She doesn't answer, so I go to the john, taking my own sweet time about it in hopes she'll cool down.

She doesn't. She's still sitting rigid when I return, her eyes glowing like a cat's, her fists curled into two pale tennis balls on the coverlet. I sit down on an uncomfortable chair and study a large crack in the wall behind the bed, waiting for the lecture to begin.

"I saw you kissing him," she accuses.

Well, listen to *her*, would you. Courtney Johnson, who's probably kissed every jock in Atherton—not to mention the ones in Palo Alto and Menlo Park—has just joined the Moral Majority.

Something else is coming into focus. If she knew I was outside on the bench kissing Lowell, she wasn't really worried that I was off by myself in hypoglycemic reaction. It *is* my friendship with Lowell she can't handle.

"So?" I say.

"So he's too old for you," she says, sounding like my mother. If my mother ever talked to me like that. Which she doesn't. Mainly because I've never given her any reason to.

"He barely turned sixteen. He's not even a year and a half older than I am."

"He'll be a senior," Court says.

"You were dating seniors when you were only a freshman," I remind her.

"That's different," she says.

"What's so different about it?"

"I knew how to handle myself."

I show my annoyance with a gusty sigh.

"And I wasn't dating scuzzbrains," she adds.

I stand up and head toward the closet to get my nightgown. "I don't pass judgment on your friends," I tell her. "I don't have to listen to this."

"Yes, you do have to listen to this. Sit down!"

Her tone is so menacing that I stand fixed, but I'm too angry to sit.

Court swings her arm in the air as if she's trying to strike me though I realize, of course, she's too far away. A wad of paper sails through the air and lands near my feet. "Read that," she says.

I lean over, pick up the paper ball, and smooth it out. Wrinkles and the dim light make the writing illegible, but I recognize the paper. It's a sheet from one of those tablets that Lowell carries. My heart pounds as I walk toward the sick glow on the night table.

Dear Chris,

It was your own fault that you got pregnant, so you'll just have to suffer the consequences. I'm not going to have anything to do with you or the baby either. . . .

I feel winded. A great watermelon has burgeoned in my chest, crowding out my heart, lungs, even my voice. "Where did you get this?" I ask faintly.

"Scott found it in the wastebasket in their room. It isn't the first letter Lowell has written to her. Scott figured out a long time ago that Lowell had a girlfriend at home who was pregnant."

I'm too stunned to speak, but I think I read sympathy on Court's face. She stands up and puts her arms around me. "I know how you feel, honey. Scott and I debated for a long time whether or not we should tell you. But when you started acting so serious about him, we decided it was time we tried to protect you."

No matter how things look, I can't believe that Lowell is the sort of person who could get a girl pregnant and then abandon her.

My heart tells me that Scott and Courtney have jumped to conclusions and that there's another explanation for that letter. Besides, Scott has no business reading other people's mail, no matter where he finds it.

On the other hand, Courtney does seem to be trying to help me, and it's a cinch she knows more about these things than I do.

Maybe the best thing to do is to ask Lowell directly, face-to-face.

If he decides to tell me the truth—if I feel satisfied with his explanation—maybe I'll even tell him about my diabetes.

LOWELL
Monday, August 12, 5:45 a.m.
Hotel, Windermere

45

Jane

Cut off from family, friends, enduring grief
From mother's death and father's willful ways,
Bearing pain that offers no relief,
I fly abroad to suffer English days.
With stomach always empty but too filled,
I try to bide the clanging in my head
Of beating anvil that will not be stilled
And throbs its morning message: dread, dread, dread.
Then at last when earth holds nothing fair,
I look above my sights to gentle Jane,
Spanning with her calm the pale, gray air,
A prismed arc appearing after rain.
So now I count the gifts she's given me:
Laughter, wisdom, love, eternity.

Dear Mr. Stringham,
  What would you think of illustrating some of the poems in the literary magazine with photographs? This girl I told you about has dynamite ideas. I wish she lived in Scottsdale. . . .

As the two Canadian tourists who have been sharing the laundromat with us go out the door, Lowell faces me. "Okay, Jane. Let's have it. What's eating you?"

"Nothing's eating me."

"Look, Jane, last night, on that bench outside our hotel, you acted as if you liked me a little. Today on the boat ride you wouldn't even hold my hand. Either you're mad at me or you're playing games. If you're mad, I want to know why so we can straighten it out. But I'll tell you right now. I can't handle it if you're going to play games."

I study my fingernails. They need filing. "Maybe—maybe you're too old for me."

"That's true. I am pretty old. Sixteen. Terribly worldly."

"I guess you've dated lots of girls."

"Not too many. Three or four hundred maybe."

The washing machine I'm leaning against makes a strange new sound and begins vibrating. I stand up straighter, prepared to be firm. "I guess we can't talk if you're going to be sarcastic. I was hoping you might be honest with me."

He kicks the leg of the wooden bench and jams his thumbs in the pockets of his jeans. "Okay, expunge the record. Delete back to 'Let's have it, Jane. What's eating you?' "

"I want to know about Chris," I say.

"Chris?" He seems honestly dazzled that I should know about a Chris. "Chris *who*?"

"The Chris you write all those letters to. How many Chrises are there in your life?"

"Just one that matters, I guess."

I turn away, feeling dizzy. "So Courtney was right."

Roughly he grabs my shoulders and spins me around. "Right about what?"

His gray eyes are so intense, so searing I have to look down. "Courtney says you're too—experienced for me."

"Look, I don't give a turtle's egg what Courtney thinks. I want to know what Jane thinks. Does Jane think I'm too 'experienced' for her?"

"Maybe. I don't know very much about you, Lowell. All you've really told me is that you'll be a senior this year and you're going to edit your literary magazine. You haven't told me anything about your family. Or that girl—Chris—you're always writing to."

Lowell slams the lid of an empty washing machine. "I don't want to talk about Chris to anyone. Even you."

"I—I was hoping you'd want to explain this," I say, holding out the letter Courtney gave me last night.

With a sneer Lowell snatches it from me, looks at it briefly, then crumples it in one hand. "Where did you get that?"

"Scott found it in your wastebasket. He and Courtney thought I should know about it."

Lowell snorts. "Good old Scott. I might have guessed that he was in on this somewhere. That cretin just can't keep his hands off other people's mail. He had no business reading that. Or showing it to you."

"I know. But since I *did* read it, Lowell, I was hoping you liked me well enough to explain what it means."

"And I was hoping you liked me well enough to trust me."

Without realizing it, I'm tearing the cardboard from an empty box of soap to bits. "I'd like to trust you, but you won't give me any reasons why I should. You won't tell me who Chris is or if you're the—"

He kicks the wheel of a laundry cart with the toe of his Puma. "I haven't done anything I'm ashamed of, if that's what you mean. Unless wishing Chris were dead is a crime. I've spent a lot of time wishing that the last year, but I never got around to doing anything about it. The only person I made fairly serious plans to kill was myself."

"Lowell!" I cry.

"Oh brother, that was sure a dumb thing to admit. Now you know for sure what a wacko I am."

"You don't really mean that, do you? About wanting to kill yourself?"

He empties the coins from his pocket to the top of an empty washing machine, singling out the ten-pence pieces he'll need for the dryer and studying them as he speaks. "Not lately. Not since I've met you."

I don't speak, hoping he'll go on.

"I'm still not ready to talk about it—even to you, Jane—but I'll tell you just this much. I've had a terrible problem this past year that Chris has been a big part of. It got to the point where I just couldn't deal with things anymore and desperately wanted to die. But you've made me start trusting people again. You've made me think I can go back home and handle my problems. He turns around to face me. "I know that sounds melodramatic and pretty sicko." He shrugs. "But that's just the way things are."

"What did Chris do?" I ask.

"I really can't talk about it anymore, Jane. Honest."

JANE
Monday, August 12, 5:20 p.m.
Hotel, Windermere

47

Dressed in her ratty bathrobe, Court dries her hair with a towel as she quizzes me about Lowell. "Didn't he tell you *anything?*" she asks.

"Only that he hasn't done anything he's ashamed of."

"And you believe a barfy explanation like that?"

"I trust him, Court."

She drops her wet towel on a chair, and gets her hair blower from the bureau. "Well, don't say Scott and I didn't try to warn you."

"You don't need to warn me about him, Court. He's a wonderful person. I really like him."

She sighs. "Have you told him yet about your diabetes?"

I pick at an uneven fingernail. "No."

"He'll find out sooner or later. You should be the one to tell him. So don't put me in the position where I have to do it. Because I will if there's any more making out until eleven o'clock. I want you in bed every night by ten."

"Oh Court-ney!"

"I mean it, Jane. Ten o'clock."

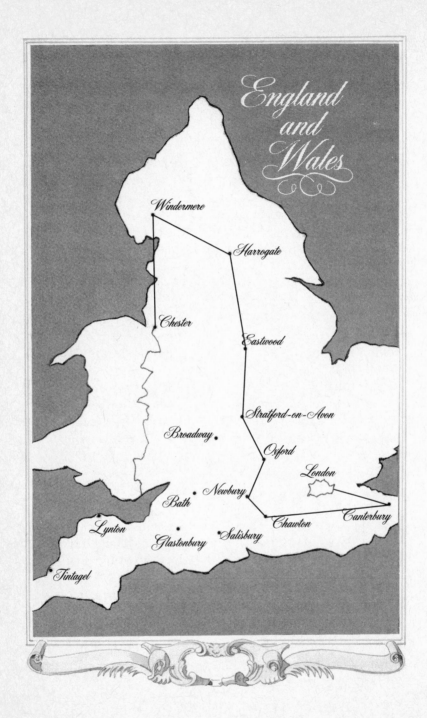

England
and
Wales

Windermere

Harrogate

Chester

Eastwood

Stratford-on-Avon

Broadway

Oxford

London

Newbury

Bath

Canterbury

Lynton

Chawton

Glastonbury   Salisbury

Tintagel

You'd think we'd be used to English downpours after two weeks, but Lowell and I still carry our western U.S. instincts. When the heavens unload on Chester, we spring for the nearest cover we can find, which happens to be a boutique specializing in leather accessories.

Several members of our tour are already inside. Glenna Feinstein is making faces in a mirror as she tries on a floppy-brimmed hat that seems half as big as she is. Courtney and Scott are considering his-and-her belts with enormous silver buckles. Dr. Phillips is studying a black handbag as if he wants to make sure the cow that contributed its hide didn't die from oversize pores.

He holds it up for our view and smiles broadly. "What do you think of it?"

"For you?" Lowell asks.

I know he's joking, of course, but Old Hen hasn't met this side of Lowell's personality. "No, no," he assures us. "For Sylvia. It's our twenty-fifth wedding anniversary on Friday, and I want to get her something really nice. Do you think she'll like this?"

The shopkeeper sends me a look that I translate as something between hope and desperation.

"Oh, I'm sure she will," I say.

"It's dynamite," Lowell agrees. "That purse has her name written all over it. See." He traces invisible writing. "It says, 'Sylvia Phillips.' "

Old Hen lets out a drafty sigh and turns to the saleswoman. "I'll take it."

He pays for it and the saleswoman starts to put it in a plastic bag, but Old Hen has a different idea. "Can you gift-wrap it for me?" he asks.

"Of course," she says in her clipped accent. "Our boxes and paper are in the back room. I'll just be gone a bit."

The shop bell tinkles, and we all look toward the door, through which an East Indian couple has just entered.

"I'm in no hurry," Old Hen tells the saleswoman. "You go wait on those people first."

"But—"

Dr. Phillips shows her the flat of his palm. "I insist."

As she shrugs and walks toward the new customers, Old Hen invites Lowell and me into a huddle. "In our family it's considered bad luck to give anyone an empty handbag. Besides, I was planning to give Sylvia a little extra spending money for our anniversary. But I didn't want that saleslady to see me put it in the purse. She might be tempted to take it out when she goes in the back room to wrap this up." He takes a hundred-pound note from his wallet and puts it in a fitted coin purse inside the handbag. "There. No one will ever know."

He's wrong on that one. Glenna Feinstein knows. She's laid her hat on the counter and is staring open-mouthed.

"Actually, friends, I am in kind of a hurry. Sylvia will get suspicious if I'm gone too long. Jane, I wonder if you'd mind waiting for the package and keeping it for me until Friday. Sylvia will be sure to find it if it's in our room."

"Sure," I say. I'm in no hurry to go out in that rain.

He pats my arm. "Thank you." Then he leans forward, in that businesslike way of his, and walks over to the saleslady. "I just remembered that I have to go to the bank. But these young people are on a tour with me and they'll wait for my package."

The door tinkles open, and we get another blast of that heavy, wet odor that I've come to associate with England. Rain pounds onto the pavement and bounces back. But Old Hen scarcely hesitates. He raises his umbrella, scrunches his shoulders, and marches off into the elements. I stare after him, watching the determined thrust of his spine.

"Is he gone?"

I turn around and see Teresa's head poking out from the curtain of a dressing room.

"Yeah," says Glenna. "Would you believe that old tightwad is giving Sylvia a handbag with a hundred-pound note in it?"

Teresa ignores the newsflash about Old Hen and flings the curtain aside. "Ta-DAH!"

She's wearing a leather halter that's so skimpy it makes your basic bikini top look like protective armor. Just two little circles of brown about the size of doughnut holes which are magically held to the front of her with criss-crossed thongs.

I sense Lowell's eyes dilating. He suddenly turns his back to all of us and pretends total absorption in a street map of Chester. But he's having trouble with his concentration. Every now and then he sneaks another look in the direction where Teresa, barely clad, is preening before a three-way mirror.

Scott's reaction is more open. He sets down the belt he was examining and charges over. *"In tune!"* he tells Teresa.

She bites her lip, thwarting a tiny smile.

Courtney scowls.

Now the shopkeeper, who has just lost her Indian customers, sees new hope for a sale. "My, my, dearie. You look lovely."

"I'll take it," Teresa says.

"Aren't you cold?" Court suggests.

Glenna is trying on a leather vest that hangs almost to her knees. "Teresa never gets cold."

"Well, I don't suppose that's the outfit you'd choose to wear today, though, dear," says the saleswoman, looking toward the window, "even though it does seem to be clearing a little. I'll just go gift-wrap this package for the gentleman while you slip into your blouse. I'll be with you in a bit."

When Teresa and the saleslady go their separate ways, Lowell shows me the places on his map he thinks we should walk to. The Roman ruins. The bell tower. The cathedral. We're discussing where to go first when the saleslady comes back with Old Hen's package. Hideous wrapping paper with purple flowers, but why should I care? She puts it into a plastic bag to protect it from the rain, and Lowell and I start toward the door.

Court blocks our path, beaming her Miss Winsome America smile at Lowell. "Would you mind being Scott's buddy for the rest of the day? I have something important to discuss with Jane. Family business. You understand."

Before Lowell can answer, Court takes my arm and escorts me out the door.

"What's the matter?" I ask. "Did something happen to Mom and Dad? Courtney, what is it?"

She looks around to see if anyone's following us.

"Oh, it's that *infantile* Scott. He's absolutely the *dullest* person I've ever met in my life. For two whole weeks I've tried to help him out by being friendly to him, but I'm going to barf if I have to spend another single minute with him. Anyway, I've done more than my share. Let some other girl play Do Gooder for a change. Teresa maybe." She turns back in the direction of the leather boutique with a sneer. "I bet she even *eats* those Beef and Bun hamburgers."

JANE
Tuesday, August 13, 8:10 p.m.
Hotel, Chester

49

While Lowell goes to borrow Ryan's Scrabble board, I wait for him in the unheated lobby of our hotel, thumbing through *Chester, Heritage City Official Guide*, which I picked up in a shop near the cathedral earlier today.

Someone *clip-clops* up to me in high heels. "Don't say I didn't tell you," says Teresa.

"Huh?" I say, looking up. She tells me so many things it's usually hard to keep the entries straight.

"You know."

"No, I don't," I say with a shiver. Just looking at Teresa makes me feel cold. She's wearing an off-the-shoulder T-shirt and high-heeled sandals with no stockings. I warm my own feet by slipping off my shoes and curling them up under me.

"Think," she insists. Telling me to think is her favorite occupation, though I'm not actually crazy about these guessing games.

"I can't."

"Yes, you can. What did I tell you the first time we met? Right on the top of that double-decker bus from Heathrow Airport to our hotel?"

The scene starts focusing. "You told me to call you Teresa, not Lucy Beth."

"Yes and what else?"

"You told me that you were the only student from Carrington Academy that Dr. Phillips had recruited for this tour."

"But what *else*? What did I tell you about Courtney and Scott?"

"You told me that they were pushers. And that their romance wouldn't last until the end of the tour."

"Well, was I right or was I right?"

"Oh, I don't know." I close my *Official Guide* and set it on the worn carpet, next to my shoes. "They may have had a little problem this afternoon, but I wouldn't exactly say—"

"Little problem! I'd love to hear your definition of nuclear war. Courtney has been telling everyone that Scott is the scuzziest human being she's ever met in her life, and Scott has been telling everyone that Courtney is out of tune." Teresa takes a scrungy brush from her shoulder bag and fluffs the yellow frizz on her head.

"Everyone has fights now and then. They'll forget all about it tomorrow. As soon as they get on the bus."

"No, they won't. You'll find out. Ryan has already asked Courtney to be his buddy tomorrow. And Karen has already asked Scott." Teresa sits down beside me on the sofa and gestures impatiently with her hairbrush. "Don't you think that was a stinking thing of Karen to do?"

"What?" I say with a sigh. Another guessing game.

"Asking Scott to be her buddy before I'd even heard about the breakup." She stands up again. "Well, it won't do her any good. We have two hundred and eighty pounds in the pot for my new contest, and I'm going to win it this time. I'm going to be the next girl who's asked to be some boy's buddy."

I look up at her frizzy hair, her crooked nose, her pathetic outfit—and feel this terrible urge to stroke her head. The way you'd try to comfort a lost puppy.

JANE
Wednesday, August 14, 7:16 a.m.
Tour bus, Chester

50

Glenna, who's too short to see us in the usual way, kneels on the seat in front of us and turns around to talk to Lowell and me. "Can you believe this weather? Seven rainy days out of the last eight."

We're sitting in our bus in front of the hotel, ready to leave for Broadway. Our suitcases have been wedged into the luggage compartment, most of us are in our seats, and the driver has long since started the engine—wasting gasoline and spewing noxious fumes on Chester's famous City Road. The thing missing is Teresa, Glenna's buddy for the day. So far she's sixteen minutes late.

You can look at the face of Dr. Time-Is-Money Phillips, who's pacing back and forth just outside the bus, and imagine the mathematical computations going on in his head. Sixteen minutes times 41 people equals 10.9 hours, not to mention the bus driver and the gasoline, which don't come cheap these days. Old Hen seems ready to wrestle a grizzly bear.

Cripes! Speaking of bare, Teresa walks toward the bus wearing her doll-sized halter. In weather that can't be fifty degrees Fahrenheit.

As soon as she's close enough to hear him, Scott lets out a whistle. Naturally, everyone crowds to the windows to see what he's so excited about. And once they find out, most of the guys join in on a regular stereophonic chorus of blowing and tooting.

Old Hen's face turns as purple as a plum. There's too much commotion on the bus, and I'm too far from the action to hear the exact dialogue, but I can figure out the gist of it from what I see.

First the driver shuts off the engine and steps outside the bus.

Then Old Hen takes off his jacket and puts it on Teresa. (I've never seen him in shirt sleeves before, and without a coat on he seems almost as naked as she was.)

Then Old Hen and Teresa stand dripping in the rain (where's Old Hen's umbrella, for heaven's sake?) while the bus driver opens the luggage compartment and starts pulling out the bags.

Then Teresa picks up one of them and heads back toward the hotel.

Then inside the bus the whistles and cheers for Teresa turn to boos and catcalls for Old Hen.

Finally, Dr. Phillips storms in the door and seizes the microphone. "That's enough, friends!" he rasps, like someone in the middle of an asthma attack. "I don't want to hear another remark from anyone. The next person I hear referring to this incident will be severely punished."

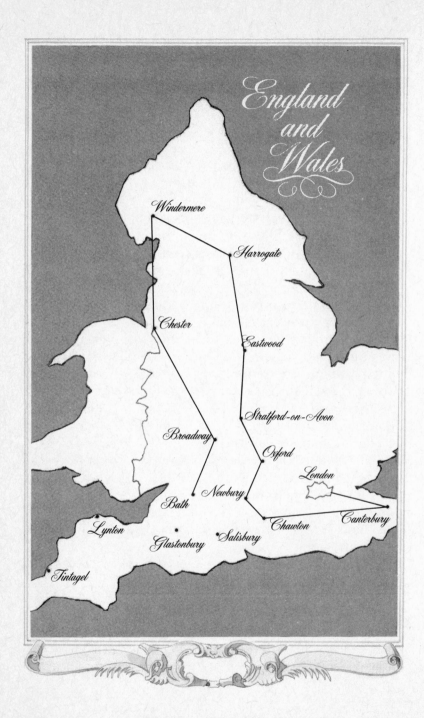

England
and
Wales

Windermere

Harrogate

Chester

Eastwood

Stratford-on-Avon

Broadway

Oxford

London

Newbury

Bath

Chawton

Canterbury

Lynton

Glastonbury

Salisbury

Tintagel

"Well, friends, the baths you just visited are one of the real showplaces of the British Isles. The natural hot springs were discovered by the Romans during the occupation of England nearly two thousand years ago. And the baths they built are the best-preserved Roman ruins in England."

We're standing here shivering in a public park about half a mile from the baths while Old Hen repeats everything the guide already told us inside. He figures he should give us a rerun of the entire tour just in case anyone was suffering from temporary deafness while we were going through the building.

Most of the kids are whispering or looking at the postcards they've just bought. Glenna Feinstein is jogging in place about thirty feet from the rest of us. Teresa stands off in another direction, chewing a fingernail. She hasn't been herself since her public humiliation yesterday, and I'm worried about her. I decide to go talk to her.

"I like that blouse," I tell her.

Teresa doesn't answer, just studies the nail she has chewed and then chews it again.

"I haven't seen you wear it before. Is it new?"

"No."

"You should wear it more often. Aqua looks good on you."

Teresa spits out the nail she has just chewed. "You know what I *wanted* to wear."

Since she's brought up the subject herself, I decide it's safe for me to talk about it. "I'm sorry about what happened yesterday," I tell her. Teresa keeps on chewing, so I try again. "Old Hen wasn't very tactful. I know just how you feel."

"You do not." She spits out another piece of nail with the words. "You have a boyfriend. You and Courtney have hogged all the boys on this tour. No one understands how I feel."

"Well, maybe I don't understand exactly how you feel. But I've had embarrassing things happen to me, too."

"In public? In front of forty kids?"

I think about the three most humiliating experiences of my life. The three times I had hypoglycemic reactions in public. Once during a horse show when I went to see Court perform. Once on the BART subway going into San Francisco. And once in the hall at school. Every time there were huge crowds of people present to see me yell and throw things and act like a lunatic before I finally passed out. The time at school was the worst, though, because the people who watched me were kids my own age. The hardest thing I ever did in my life was going back to school the next day.

I nod. "More than forty. It was in the hall at school. Between classes."

"What happened?" she challenges. "Just what happened?"

Too late I realize I shouldn't have started this. Here I've spent the last two weeks trying to keep Court from telling these kids about me, and now I've spilled the beans to the biggest blabbermouth on the tour. Quickly I try to think of another embarrassing experience that happened to me at school.

"Go on," Teresa insists.

"Well," I begin, wondering if the story I'm about to tell will really sound embarrassing enough. Compared to the hypoglycemic reactions it was a real nothing. A positive zilch. "There's this jock at our school who thinks he's Mr. Wonderful."

"Hmmph. I bet Courtney thinks he is, too."

"He's only fourteen. Too young for Court to notice. Anyhow, she's already in high school. She's two years ahead of me."

"Well, go on." Teresa must be feeling better. She stops chewing her fingernails and unwraps a ball of bubble gum.

From the corner of my eye I see Glenna standing on her hands on the wet grass and scissoring her size 3½ feet back and forth in the air. Old Hen scowls at her, then looks over at Teresa and me and scowls even harder.

Teresa lobs the gum ball into her mouth and begins to chew. "Are you going to tell me or aren't you?" she asks me thickly.

I'm nervous about the way Old Hen is glaring at us. "Dr. Phillips is trying to talk now," I whisper. "I'll tell you later."

"I want to hear right now," Teresa says. "I'm not afraid of the Ayatollah." To prove her point she sticks out her tongue at Old Hen as soon as he looks the other way.

Dr. Phillips raises the volume of his lecture. "Bath was rebuilt in the eighteenth century, and it became the most fashionable place in England. Wealthy parents would bring their unmarried daughters here to meet eligible suitors."

Realizing Teresa won't let me off the hook until I tell her my story, I begin, keeping my voice as low as I can. "Well, this dumb jock I told you about came up to me in the hall and pretended he wanted help with an algebra problem. While we were standing there looking at his book he was pinning a picture on my back. A really raunchy picture from some magazine like *Penthouse*. Kids started laughing and pointing at me and making crude remarks. But I didn't have any idea what the joke was. I walked clear across the building and upstairs to my French class before I discovered what had happened."

Already the size of a Texas grapefruit, a pink bubble balloons in front of Teresa's face. I can't read her expression behind it, but I have the feeling she isn't impressed by my story.

"I was so embarrassed I could have died," I explain. Your basic exaggeration. Lots worse things have happened to me.

At last the bubble bursts and Teresa speaks. "That wouldn't have embarrassed me."

"Maybe not. I guess everyone wouldn't be embarrassed by something like that. But lots of people would be, even some boys I know."

"Among the things Bath is famous for is its exquisite Georgian architecture," Old Hen continues. "We're now going to get in the bus and drive past the Royal Crescent and Queen's Square. But I've decided to make this part of the tour optional. Some of you have been complaining about the lack of free time to go shopping or do your washing, so I'll excuse anyone who would like to do something else this afternoon."

Teresa raises a hand. "Do we have to stick with our buddies?"

"Of course," says Old Hen. Then maybe he decides he's been hard enough on Teresa for awhile and reconsiders. He clears his throat. "Check with your buddies and see what they want to do. If you can't agree, you can find another pair of buddies and go with them. But no one can go off alone. The only place you can go alone is back to your room. I'll have the bus driver drop off anyone at the hotel who wants to go there."

There's a general hubbub while kids talk to their buddies. Even though it's been three days since we used the laundromat in Windermere, Lowell and I decide we want to go on the bus ride to see the city. Teresa wants to go back to the hotel and wash her hair.

As the bus pulls up to the hotel to let people off, Teresa seems agitated. Her roommate, Karen, has gone shopping with Scott and isn't on the bus. And Teresa has forgotten to bring her hotel key. "Would it be all right if I used your room to wash my hair?" she asks.

"Sure," I say and hand her my key.

JANE
Friday, August 16, 11:20 a.m.
Outside the hotel, Salisbury

52

The sky's the color of robin's eggs. The sun bounces off trees and vines, turning each leaf into hundreds of shades of green.

I couldn't be more excited. We've arrived here in Salisbury, the place where Eleanor of Aquitaine was kept under house arrest for fifteen years and one of the cities I've really looked forward to visiting on this trip. Today we'll be seeing some of the places Eleanor visited on her daily rides, including Stonehenge and Salisbury Cathedral.

The day is special in another way, too. The letter of instructions we received from Old Hen long ago told us that the price of the tour included only two meals a day, breakfast and dinner. But because today is his twenty-fifth wedding anniversary, we're having lunch "on the house." He's spread word secretly among the kids to meet in the hotel dining room at noon. It's a big surprise for Sylvia.

Right now we're still on the bus in the tiny courtyard of the hotel, waiting for the maids to get our rooms ready because we've thrown off the hotel's timing by arriving before noon. On the bus we've already seen our mail, and most of the kids are getting restless.

Lowell teases me by grabbing my mail. (He never gets any of his own. That's one thing I still don't understand about him.) Another dumb postcard from Brenda. The sixth. I know Lowell well enough now that it doesn't bother me for him to see it, even though it's just like all the others she's sent. Tacky.

He looks at the picture, then turns it over to read the message: *Dear Jane, I'm breathlessly waiting for details of all your conquests. What's it like to make out in England?*

Lowell hands the postcard back, a sly smile on his lips.

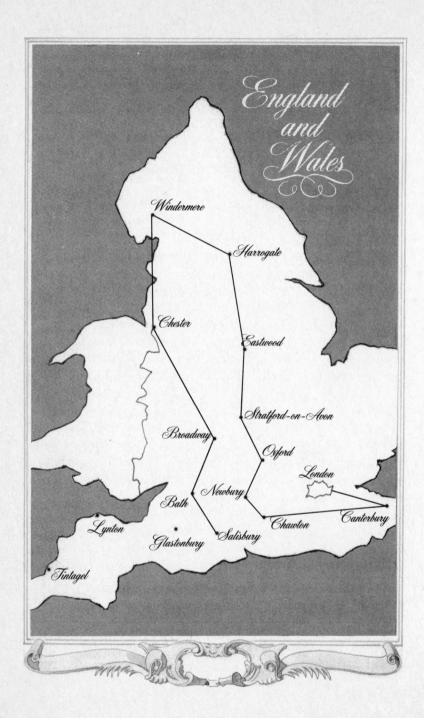

England
and
Wales

Windermere
Harrogate
Chester
Eastwood
Stratford-on-Avon
Broadway
Oxford
London
Newbury
Bath
Chawton
Canterbury
Lynton
Salisbury
Glastonbury
Tintagel

"Women! Look, is that all you talk about when you get together—making out?"

I consider that question. "Not really. I don't think we talk about it as much as guys do."

Lowell's smile broadens to a laugh. "Touché!"

JANE
Friday, August 16, 12:40 p.m.
Dining room, hotel, Salisbury

53

We've just finished lunch, and Sylvia's making a big production out of opening the present in the ugly purple paper. She's determined to untie the knot instead of slipping off the ribbon as any sensible person would. I wish she'd get on with it so the rest of us could get on with what we really came to Salisbury for—to see Stonehenge and the cathedral.

Sitting on her left, Old Hen smiles indulgently.

Sitting on her right, Merrill Bickerstaff looks bored. "Here, I'll help you." He opens a pocket knife and attacks the ribbon like a surgeon. *Snip.*

Sylvia's mouth drops open. Maybe she was going to save that ribbon for her scrapbook. Maybe she was going to sleep with it under her pillow. Anyhow, she opens the rest of the package faster.

"Oh Henry," she coos, "it's just what I wanted. It's lovely."

He needs more assurance. "You like it? You really like it?"

"Oh yes, it's beautiful." She kisses him lightly on the cheek.

"Why don't you open it?" Old Hen urges her. "Maybe there's something inside."

Sylvia does as she's told and begins unfolding a large

piece of paper she finds in the handbag. The look on her face changes to horror. "Henry!" she reproves.

"Not that! I didn't put that there. Look inside the zipper."

She burrows again and pulls out the hundred-pound note. But before she can show it to the rest of us, Merrill has already seen the first object and is holding it up for general view. A huge centerfold from some raunchy magazine.

Whistling and cheering erupt from everywhere. "Nice going, Old Hen," someone calls out.

Smoke is practically billowing from his nostrils as Old Hen stands up and bangs his water glass with a spoon. "Stop that, friends. Stop it this instant."

Silence.

We've never seen him this angry. Not even when Merrill and Ryan held the bus up forty-five minutes. Not even when Teresa tried to wear her skimpy halter in the rain. Today is Old Hen's twenty-fifth wedding anniversary and probably the first time in his career of conducting student tours to Europe that he's ever provided lunch "on the house." And now we've embarrassed Sylvia and spoiled his special surprise party for her.

"Jane," he says. "Come here."

My heart pounds. My legs feel like noodles.

"You of all people," he says when I finally get there. His eyes burn me like hot coals. "I certainly wouldn't have expected this of you. How could you do such a thing?"

No wonder the kids at Carrington dislike this man. He has no right to humiliate me this way in front of everyone, especially since I'm innocent. I glance hopefully toward Teresa who is busy looking in a mirror as she applies a fresh coat of purple lipstick.

"I didn't—" I start to say and change my mind. Teresa should speak up, not put me in the position of acting like a coward.

"All of you friends are getting completely out of hand," Old Hen continues. "I've been very patient up to now, but I see you didn't appreciate it. I'll have to start treating you the way you deserve."

Come on, Teresa, I'm thinking. If you're really planning to become a saint some day, now's the time to start repenting.

"I'll have to make an example of you, Jane."

What can he do to me? Send a letter to my parents? Maybe he'll try to phone. For a minute I consider finking, even though I've always hated finks. Anyhow, what if Teresa didn't really do it? Just because she was already ticked off at Old Hen—just because I told her about the picture that was pinned on my back at school—just because I gave her the key to my hotel room—doesn't absolutely *prove* she's responsible. It might have been Court. Or Ryan. Or almost anyone.

"You'll be confined to your hotel room the rest of the day. You may not go on the bus tour with us this afternoon. Courtney will bring your dinner to your room. And just in case you have any plans to sneak off, I'll telephone periodically to make sure you're there. If you're not, I'll take sterner measures tomorrow."

Stay in my hotel room? In Salisbury? I clench my fists, as if that futile gesture will somehow give me strength against the quiver in my chin. I won't let this awful old man see me cry. I won't.

"All right, friends, the rest of you have twenty minutes to go to your rooms and freshen up before the bus leaves."

Court comes up wearing the Big Sister look she's been using a lot lately. "Can I do anything for you, honey?"

I shake my head.

"Well, I thought the joke was funny. Old Hen just has no sense of humor."

Lowell glares at her. "Jane didn't do it, Court."

I look gratefully at Lowell. "How did you know?"

He squeezes my hand. "Because I know you."

"Why didn't you tell him?" Courtney asks. "Do you know who did do it?"

"No," I fib. "Not for sure anyway."

Court shrugs and goes to the bus while Lowell walks me to my room. "Look," he says, trying to sound cheerful. "Why don't you give me your camera, and I'll take some pictures for you at Stonehenge and the cathedral?"

"Okay, but it won't be the same. I wanted to do it myself. Besides, I wanted to take your picture in all those places."

"Yeah, I know how you feel. When I saw we had a sunny day, I ran down the street a couple of minutes ago and blew two hundred and fifty pounds on a camera of my own so I could take pictures of you."

JANE
Friday, August 16, 4:15 p.m.
Hotel, Salisbury

54

Of all the rooms that Court and I have shared on this tour, this one's the most depressing. No bigger than our kitchen pantry at home. Faded green carpet with seams coming undone. Uneven floor that squeaks when you walk on it. Almost no illumination, even on this sunny day.

Sitting on the bed (there's nowhere else, except the floor), I've spent the last three hours looking through my Monarch Notes and guidebooks and skimming through the Jane Austen books I've already read. Old Hen has telephoned once. The highlight of my afternoon.

My back aches from sitting without a back rest. My legs ache from sitting Indian style. Even my cramps are getting cramps. And this lumpy mattress, which is bigger than the bed frame it's resting on, lurches toward the floor if I move about suddenly.

I'm bored. Not to mention feeling sorry for myself.

Convinced that I'm entitled, I try to call up the tears I fought back earlier. But they're bored, too. What a terrible way to waste a beautiful afternoon. And in *England*.

Careful not to dislodge the mattress, I get up, stretch, and look out the tiny (also dirty) window. So this is the Salisbury I looked forward to coming to. An old courtyard! I try to make ironic comparisons between myself and Eleanor of Aquitaine, who was also under house arrest here. Maybe the joke will amuse me someday, but today it isn't funny.

To liven up my afternoon I go into the bathroom and drink a glass of lukewarm water.

Now what?

Besides the bed, the chest of drawers, and the night table (on which rest a telephone and a lamp with a forty-watt bulb, your basic English decor), there is only one other furnishing in this room. It's a tiny hotplate/sideboard permanently mounted on the wall, like the hotplates in all of the other hotel rooms where we've stayed so far. Up till now I haven't paid much attention to the English custom of afternoon tea, but today—because I'm bored— I make my way between the bed and the wall to examine the goodies.

On the mini-sideboard are all the necessary provisions for making coffee, tea, or hot chocolate. More important, there are also four cookies (biscuits?), individually wrapped: two shortbread and two chocolate-covered wafers.

I pick up one of the chocolate wafers and sniff at it through the blue wrapper. Yum. I've always loved chocolate, but it's been a no-no since I was nine years old. I sniff again. Heaven.

Smelling something can't hurt me, Dr. Lieberman. I decide my nostrils deserve a closer whiff on a rotten day like this. I remove first the blue paper and then the foil, more careful than Sylvia was when she unwrapped her handbag. These wrappings, after all, must be preserved for reuse.

Mmmm! Ecstasy!

Well, why not eat it? Don't I deserve something today?

I gobble it quickly, tearing the wrapper into tiny pieces and flushing them down the toilet so Courtney won't suspect.

Before I realize what's happening, I've consumed three more cookies and two cups of hot chocolate and flushed the evidence down the toilet.

I don't feel a thing. It didn't hurt a bit. So there, Dr. Lieberman, you were wrong. I don't look dead, do I?

Something about that word shocks me into reality. Just how big an overdose *will* kill me? And how soon? Dr. Lieberman never got down to specifics.

Flashing through my mind is a TV special I saw last year. Girls who gorged themselves on too much food and then (to lose weight, not necessarily to stay alive) forced themselves to vomit. I rush back to the bathroom and do the necessary deed.

Disgusting.

With wet balls of toilet paper I clean up the bottom of the toilet seat and the floor, more revulsed at myself than at the foul-smelling splatters. I realize belatedly that the cookies didn't taste all that good going down, either, not as good as they smelled.

Weakly I sink to the bed, trying to sort out the terrible things I have done. Eating the rich food was bad enough. But if Dr. Lieberman ever explained to me what vomiting will do, I wasn't listening. And I need to know. I need to know right now.

Oh, Dr. Lieberman, I need you. Why aren't you here?

The sound of Courtney's key in the lock wakes me up, and I turn over.

"You okay?" she asks.

"Yeah," I say, remembering my recent orgy. I hope I'm okay. I sure hope I'm okay. I lift up on an elbow to look at her. "Start from the beginning and tell me all about Salisbury Cathedral and Stonehenge."

"All right." She sits down on the bed beside me, still playing Big Sister. "But first for the News of the Day. Guess who won the two hundred and eighty pounds in Teresa's second big popularity contest?"

"Teresa," I guess bitterly. Isn't that just how cruddy life can be sometimes? Not only do I get punished for Teresa's crime, but she wins two hundred and eighty pounds besides.

Court shakes her head. "Nope. Merrill split the pot with Marjean Axelson."

I sit up for real now. "Merrill? He wasn't in the contest. It was just for girls."

"Oh, really, Jane. Don't be naive. You don't really think you can keep a thing like that a secret, do you? The guys have known about it all along. They've just been waiting for some girl to hint she might be willing to split the pot before they asked her to be a buddy."

"How did the guys find out about the contest? What girl would fink about a thing like that?"

Courtney suddenly doesn't look at me anymore. She opens her shoulder bag and gets out a nail file. "How should I know?"

"You seem to know everything else, though. *You* told, didn't you?" I accuse.

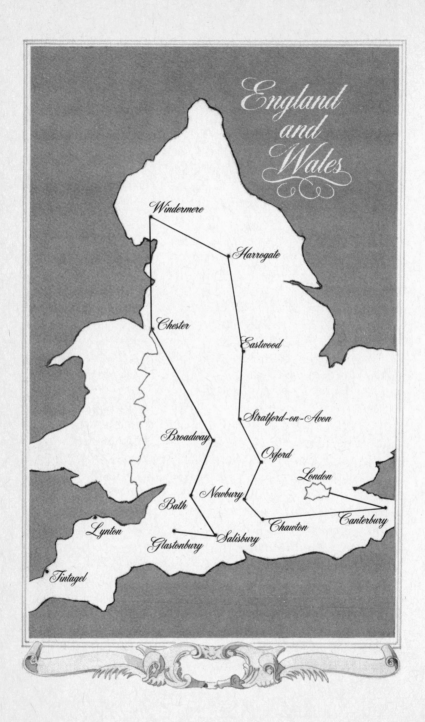

England
and
Wales

Windermere

Harrogate

Chester

Eastwood

Stratford-on-Avon

Broadway

Oxford

London

Newbury

Canterbury

Bath

Chawton

Lynton

Salisbury

Glastonbury

Tintagel

The file makes an unpleasant noise against Court's fingernail. "Wel-l-l-l, Scott and I discussed lots of things while we were going together. It's possible we discussed that. But why should you care? You and I weren't in the contest anyway."

It strikes me that Courtney may be right. It's possible that I'm getting too worked up about a principle that when violated almost makes up for my incarceration this afternoon.

JANE
Saturday, August 17, 10:55 a.m.
Glastonbury Abbey
56

Glastonbury Abbey proves to be an unexpected bonus.

We find out after we get here that Eleanor of Aquitaine spent almost as much time here as she did at Stonehenge. It was at this church, in fact, that some of Eleanor's workmen found an impressive tomb bearing the remains of a tall man and woman. Eleanor decided right away that the tomb belonged to King Arthur and Queen Guinevere. Eleanor convinced everyone who mattered, and a few years later (in 1276) Edward I ordered that the bodies be reinterred in front of the High Altar. Don't ask me how Eleanor knew so much about people who lived six hundred years before she did. Eleanor had lots of talents that the rest of us don't understand.

Aside from the interesting history, the grounds are beautiful. Some of the abbey walls, or portions of them, still stand. And in a couple of places the intricate mosaic floor of the church has been preserved under wooden lids that tourists can lift up to see the floor. Most of the area is now overgrown with grass, though, and the grounds outside the abbey are planted with lush shrubs.

You can't help being impressed by this site, even if you haven't read *A Proud Taste for Scarlet and Miniver* five times and aren't a big Eleanor of Aquitaine fan.

Lowell and I take pictures as if film is being outlawed tomorrow. *Click, click. Snap, snap.* The marker telling about the burial of Arthur and Guinevere. The remaining portions of the floor. The crumbling walls. The bushes and trees.

Then Lowell takes pictures of me standing by all those places. Then I take the same pictures of him. Then we ask strangers to take pictures of both of us standing together.

We've run out of film but we still have a few minutes before we have to meet the bus, so we sit down on the grass together.

"Until you've seen them with your own eyes, you don't really believe all those shades of green on English postcards," Lowell says.

"Um-hmm," I agree.

I sit silently beside him, not wanting to bring up the fact that our trip's nearly over. Just one and a half more days of sightseeing. Then the long, full day's ride back to London so we can catch our plane to Chicago. Not quite three days total. End of summer romance. End of Lowell. Blackout. Zilch.

Why doesn't he suggest we write to each other? Please, Lowell. Please, ask me to write to you.

He picks up a flat rock and spins it off into the distance. "Well, I guess we better go back to the bus."

Darn that Chris, whoever she is!

JANE
Saturday, August 17, 3:20 p.m.
Tour bus to Lynton

57

"I have a wonderful surprise that I've been saving for you, friends," Old Hen tells us through the microphone. "This hotel where we'll be staying in Lynton has a live band that will be playing tonight. Because tomorrow is Sunday and you'll have to get up extra early the next morning for the long drive back to London, we're going to have our final party tonight. If the members of the social committee will meet me in the lobby after we've all taken our bags to our rooms, I'll give them the money I've set aside for our farewell celebration."

"No kidding," Scott says to Old Hen, looking up from a game of gin with Merrill. The two guys are sitting in the front of the bus, across the aisle from Lowell and me. "What rock group is it?"

We're in England, aren't we? Home of Culture Club and Police and Rolling Stones? Scott expects the best.

"It's a wonderful group that I heard last year when I stayed at this hotel," Old Hen replies. "They play marvelous tunes from the forties."

"The forties!" Scott complains.

"The forties!" Merrill croaks. "Shoot! Even my parents don't hardly remember the forties."

Lowell leans across the aisle to talk to them. "All the most romantic songs came from the forties. Haven't you ever heard 'Does the Spearmint Lose Its Flavor on the Bedpost Overnight?' "

Merrill groans. Scott glares.

Lowell looks back at me with a grin. "Maybe they'll even play our song."

He and I have never even danced together, much less

chosen a song, but I'm willing to along with a gag. "Mairzy Doats?" I ask.

"That's our number two song," he says.

"What's number one?"

"I'll tell you if you promise to dance with me every time they play it. And every dance in between."

I give in easily. "Okay. What is it?"

"God Save the Queen."

I grin.

"Remember, you promised," he reminds me.

"A woman of honor never breaks her promises," I say.

JANE
Saturday, August 17, 4:00 p.m.
Outside hotel, Lynton

58

Parked in front of the hotel in Lynton while we wait for Scott and Old Hen to come back to the bus with our mail and room assignments, the kids are experiencing end-of-the-tour fever. Paper airplanes are sailing back and forth above our heads. Soda pop and candy bars (forbidden on British buses) are being passed around. Ryan Donovan and Merrill Bickerstaff are singing a raunchy drinking song. And the bus driver is conferring nervously with Sylvia.

From her seat directly behind me Teresa reaches her hands over my shoulders and fans them out so I can see her ten perfectly sculptured purple fingernails. "Ta-DAH!"

It's the first word she's said to me since I took her punishment yesterday, and frankly it's the wrong one. I brush her hands away from me as if they were flies at a picnic.

She puts them right back again. "Well, what do you think?" she asks.

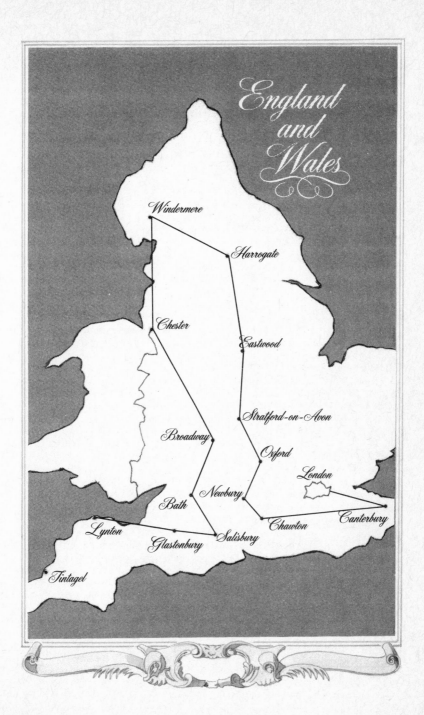

England and Wales

Windermere
Harrogate
Chester
Eastwood
Stratford-on-Avon
Broadway
Oxford
London
Newbury
Bath
Canterbury
Lynton
Chawton
Salisbury
Glastonbury
Tintagel

It occurs to me that she's acting entirely too jovial. It occurs to me that it's time someone told her off. I turn around and glare at her. "I think you owe me an apology."

Lowell, who has suddenly put two and two together, chimes in. "Are you the low-life who let Jane take the rap?"

"I mean what do you think about my new fingernails. Can you believe they're actually artificial?"

"I can believe *you're* artificial," says Lowell.

Teresa brushes the air with a limp hand. "What's the matter with you two? Can't you take a little joke? Everyone but you and Old Hen thought it was really funny. Besides, all the kids were proud of you for playing a trick on him. Actually, you should be grateful to me for letting you take the credit for my idea."

"Here comes Scott," Marjean yells, and everyone crowds toward the windows. Old Hen still seems to be in the hotel, but Scott walks back toward the bus with the mail. It doesn't look like a very big bundle.

He climbs aboard, takes the mike, and does his famous Old Hen imitation. "Well, friends, I have wonderful news for most of you. Most of you won't have to answer any letters tonight because in the long period of time that you've been gone from home all the members of your fan clubs have died from hardening of the writing apparatus. Only one person received any mail today."

"Who?" someone calls out.

Scott doesn't answer. Instead, he clutches the letter to his chest, trying to build suspense. "It seems only fair that the recipient of this letter should share it with all of us. Do I hear a motion to that effect?"

"I move," says Merrill.

"Second," says Marjean.

"NO!" I yell. Even though I'm sure the letter isn't for me, I don't think what Scott's doing is funny, and I guess I should know. Already on this trip I've (a) had my mail read aloud to the group and (b) been the butt of another "joke."

Scott doesn't wait for more objections, or a vote either, for that matter. He rips open the envelope with his right index finger, puts the mike back in front of his face, and begins reading: *"Dear Lucy Beth—"*

"Who's Lucy Beth?" Ryan yells.

"That's Teresa," Karen answers.

Scott tries again: *"Dear Lucy Beth, I'm sure you felt it strange that I seemed so eager for you to go to England this summer but I thought it would be better for you to be out of the house while your father and I were working out our problems. We've now talked things over carefully—"* Scott's voice weakens and then cracks. He's not quite sure if he should go on. *"—and have decided to get a divorce."*

"Stop it!" Teresa shrieks as she springs from her seat and races down the aisle. *"Stop it!"*

Turned crazy now, she's screaming and tearing at Scott like an alley cat. "Give me that! It's mine!"

Scott tries to ward off her blows with bent elbows but doesn't try to strike her back. "Hey, I just meant it as a joke."

"Joke! I'll show you joke." Purple talons claw the air as they try to gouge Scott's eyes, bringing blood to one cheek. Teresa's fingernails make vicious weapons, so Scott must really be hating himself to stand there and let her rip at him.

Lowell and I realize this at almost the same instant because I follow as he bounds up the aisle and seizes Teresa by the wrists, a final act of humiliation. She sinks like a glob of Jell-o into an empty seat. "You're all against me. Everyone," she sobs. Lowell steps back, dropping her wrists. This seems like my cue to move in and put my arms around her. "No one's against you, Teresa. Nothing that's happened was directed at you. You just stay here and read your letter, and the rest of us will leave you alone."

Suddenly a new emotion seizes her. She throws her arms around me and squeezes me so tight I can hardly breathe. "No, Jane, don't you leave me. I want you to stay with me while I read it. I want you to stay with me all night. Let Courtney and Karen share a room for tonight. Please, Jane. I need you. You're the best friend I've ever had."

I'm the best friend she's ever had?

Poor Teresa. Poor, poor Teresa.

JANE

Saturday, August 17, 9:45 p.m.
Hotel, Lynton

59

The musicians had car trouble on the way to the hotel, and they're still not here—at 9:45. Lowell and I have gone outside to be alone while we wait for them. He has his arm around me as we sit there on a bench in the cold.

"There you are, Jane!" Karen accuses. She seems out of breath. "Teresa's upstairs having hysterics because she says you've abandoned her, too. You've got to go to her right now."

"I told her I'd be there as soon as Lowell and I had three dances together," I say.

"That was nearly two hours ago. She doesn't believe you, and she's been taking it out on me."

I sigh. "Okay." I try to stand up, but Lowell pulls me back to him.

"Tell her Jane will be there in a few minutes," he says to Karen.

"You tell her," Karen suggests. "I've already moved my stuff to Jane's room, and I'm not going back. The kids are playing games in the lobby until the musicians arrive, and I'm going to the farewell party." She storms off.

I remove Lowell's arm from my shoulder and stand up. "I'd better go."

He stands up, too. "You promised to dance with me."

"She needs me, Lowell."

"And I don't need you?"

"She's had a bad day. It must be awful to learn your parents are getting divorced. Especially in such an embarrassing way."

"So what should I do to get your sympathy? Tell you about my bad year?"

I'm torn. I've been waiting for him to tell me about himself for nearly three weeks, but maybe this isn't the time.

He's rushing into it, though, the old bitterness back in his voice. "Tell you about my mother who died two days before my birthday in July after nearly a year in bed with leukemia? About my dad who really enjoyed her illness because it gave him a chance to get better acquainted with his sleazy secretary?"

"Oh, Lowell. Is that who Chris is? Your dad's secretary?"

"Oh, this soap opera gets even better, Jane. How about my telling you the zinger that Dad laid on me as we were driving back from the funeral? That very same day? When I hadn't even digested the news that Mom was dead? He tells me Miss Sleaze is pregnant and they're going to get married right away and go on a honeymoon to Bermuda. So how would I like to use this ticket to England that he just happens to have in his pocket?"

"He should have waited for all that. Besides upsetting you, it wasn't in very good taste."

"Not in very good taste. 'Dear Dad, Miss Proper Jane Johnson from Atherton, California, says you're not in very good taste.' That should scare the biscuits right out of him." Lowell's looking away from me, toward the garden. I guess I've really upset him.

I put my hand on his arm. "That was a stupid thing to say. I'm sorry. Please forgive me."

He turns back. "Of course I forgive you, Jane. You're not the one I'm mad at. It's Dad and Chris I'd like to get even with."

"What will that solve? Maybe you should think about trying to forgive them," I say.

"They don't deserve it. Do you know why I learned how to cook? Haven't you guessed? Dad managed to work late nearly every night—when he wasn't going on his so-called business trips. Mom never complained because she thought he had to work extra hard to pay the doctor bills. Whenever I remember that he even had *me* fooled for awhile it makes me so mad I could explode."

"See? That's what I mean. You don't always forgive people because forgiveness helps them—you forgive them because forgiveness helps you."

A breeze rustles the leaves on the monkey trees as Lowell rolls his eyes at the stars. "Platitudes. Spare me the middle-class morality. Do you know what your trouble is, Jane? You have terminal patience."

"Think about it," I tell him. "Your hatred toward them didn't make *them* want to commit suicide."

Now he gets the point. Gasping, he covers his face with his hands. Is he crying? Just in case, I put my arms around him and he grabs me with such force it takes my breath away. Yes, I'm sure he's crying. We stand there clinging to each other as I feel the tremor of his body with the sobs, the wetness of his cheeks with the tears.

For some reason, I start thinking about Teresa and the way she clung to me earlier today.

"Okay, you lovebirds, break it up," Courtney says.

Lowell does just that, but not because he's ordered to. He turns his back to both of us so she won't see he's crying.

"The party's inside," Court continues.

"We were just going in," I say, suddenly aware of the strains of "Begin the Beguine." The musicians have finally arrived.

"I'll bet," Courtney says.

So she thinks we've been making out? Who cares? "Well, I'm glad the group finally got here," I say. "Lowell and I want to dance together a few times before I go upstairs to Teresa."

"You don't have time for that now," Courtney says. "Karen says Teresa's hysterical. You've got to go to her right now."

Lowell wipes his eyes with the sleeve of his sweater and turns around to challenge Court. "Stop telling Jane what she has to do. She's old enough to make up her own mind."

Courtney's equal to any boy. "It's five minutes after ten. Jane *wants* to go upstairs now, don't you, Jane?"

The threat is obvious, so I think about what it means. Lowell's too upset tonight for any more bad news, especially from Courtney. I'll find a better time and way to tell him about my diabetes.

"Okay," I say to Courtney before turning to Lowell. "Want to walk me to Teresa's room?"

Court takes my arm. "He doesn't need to bother. *I'll* see that you get there all right."

From the corner of my eye I see Lowell kick the cement step with his shiny brown loafers.

On our way to the elevator, we pass Scott in the corridor. Courtney doesn't acknowledge him, but as he and I share a wave, I notice the deep scratches on both his cheeks.

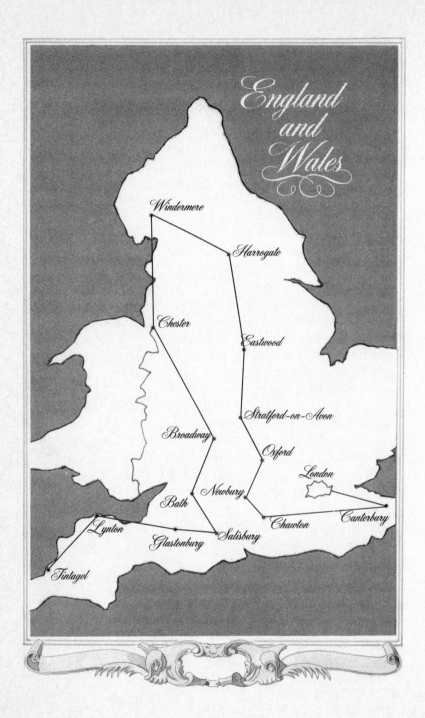

England
and
Wales

Windermere

Harrogate

Chester

Eastwood

Stratford-on-Avon

Broadway

Oxford

London

Newbury

Bath

Salisbury

Chawton

Canterbury

Lynton

Glastonbury

Tintagel

"Well, two's company, three's a crowd," Court sings gaily as she throws her cardigan on the bed.

"You mean the way Ryan acted when you told him you couldn't be his buddy today?" I ask.

"He did act a little scuzzy, didn't he? You'd think he'd realize, though, that Scott and I have been going together practically this whole trip, and it's only natural that we'd want to spend the last couple of days together."

I sit down on the straight-backed chair, take off my shoes, and curl my feet up under me. "Well, you really invite your own problems, Court. You gave Ryan a lot of encouragement for awhile. No wonder he hated being given the three's-a-crowd treatment today."

"Oh, I wasn't talking about *me*, Janie dear. I was talking about Lowell and Teresa." She bends over and pinches my cheek. "And Little Miss Popular. You should have seen the expression on your face as the two of them tried to elbow next to you on the Lynton–Lynmouth Cliff Railway and on the bus ride to Tintagel. It was hysterical."

Hysterical. Not a bad word, under the circumstances. Sometimes Courtney's right on target.

"You took your shot a long time ago," Court reminds me. "You better go to breakfast." Last day of the trip, and she's giving me the concerned-big-sister treatment. Maybe she wants to make such a good impression on me the last day that I won't remember how she's acted the rest of the time.

I take my fancy cashmere cardigan out of my suitcase and put my boring raincoat back inside, even though I know the raincoat will be more practical. "I'm not through packing," I lie. The truth is that except for being unable to make up my mind if I want to look nice or be comfortable, I've been packed for forty-five minutes, waiting for the phone to ring. (Why doesn't Lowell call?) "I keep worrying that I've forgotten something."

Unexpectedly, she puts her arm around me and gives me a squeeze. "Lowell's over his sulk by now. He's probably waiting for you in the dining room right this minute." I feel my eyes filling with tears and don't know exactly what's causing them—Court's sudden tenderness this morning or Lowell's irritation last night when I invited Teresa to play Scrabble with us after dinner. "No guy stays mad on the last day the two of you have together."

I bite my lip.

"Come on," she urges gently. "If he's not there, you can have breakfast with Scott and me. It's time you ate."

The phone rings, and I lunge for it like a woman who's just dropped a thirty-carat diamond in a sink hole.

"Hello," I pant.

"Are you up?" It's Lowell, all right, as cheerful as morning birds. Court sure understands guys better than I do.

I feel like a songbird, too. "How could anyone stay in bed the last day in England? Particularly on a day like this."

"My sentiments exactly. Are you packed?"

"Just working on it. Court's nagging me to hurry so we can go to breakfast."

"Tell her to go without you. You have a prior engagement with a dashing Knight of the Round Table."

"Lowell, do you really think King Arthur was born in Tintagel? Was that really his father's castle we saw up there on that cliff yesterday?"

"Eleanor of Aquitaine believed it. What's good enough for Eleanor is good enough for you."

I giggle. "That's right. I believe everything today."

Court shouts close enough to the phone so Lowell will hear. "You better believe I'll eat Lowell Stevens for breakfast if he doesn't hang up."

"Tell her not to worry," Lowell says. "Court can go to breakfast right now. You and I are eating every meal together today. *Alone*."

"Is it Lowell?" Court asks.

I nod.

"I told you so," she says.

I put my hand over the mouthpiece to talk to her. "Okay, Dear Abby. You go on without me. I'll be there in a minute."

Court rolls her eyes at the ceiling. "Puppy love!" She picks up her bags and heads for the door while I continue my conversation with Lowell. "Okay. I'll wait for you in the hall outside my room. Hurry."

I close my suitcase, put my share of the tip for the maid on the dresser, slip the strap of my shoulder purse over my shoulder, and grab my fancy cashmere cardigan which I've been planning to wear today. After giving the room a final once-over, I pick up my suitcase and carry-on and set them outside the door for the porter.

Lowell's in the hall almost before I am.

"I'm starving," I say. "Let's go eat."

"A hungry man is not a free man," he tells me.

"Whatever that means."

He doesn't answer, just takes my arm and guides me past the death trap of an elevator. We sail down the stairs. He's in a silly mood this morning, which makes me feel a bit giddy, too, even though I'm thinking that this may be my last chance to tell him about the diabetes.

"Lowell, you're going the wrong way. The dining room's over there."

"Man cannot live by bread alone. Woman either."

"Stop quoting people and turn around. I've got to eat," I tell him.

He opens the outside door of the hotel and nudges me gently through it. "On a day like today you want to eat Alpen in some hotel dining room? When you could be drinking dew from the wildflowers at Tintagel castle?"

"Be serious."

"Absolutely not. I forbid seriousness. You had your turn to make the rules Saturday night and Sunday and I wound up feeling sorry for myself because you chose to spend your time with Teresa. Today it's my turn to make the rules and the first one is No Seriousness. Absolutely none."

"But I have something important to tell you. And this is the first time we've been alone."

"You've noticed, too, huh?"

"Let's go sit on that bench while we talk about it," I suggest. "This may take a few minutes."

"Save it until tomorrow on the plane. Tomorrow I'll declare a Serious Discussion Day."

I shiver, partly because I'm afraid I'll lose my courage if I don't tell him about the diabetes right now, and partly because it's colder outside than it looks. I fumble with my sweater and Lowell helps me put it on.

"Okay, Guinevere," he says. "Off to the castle."

"All right. But we've got to stop at the first grocery store we come to and buy some milk and fruit or something. I'm really hungry."

"Easy. Ask me a hard one."

We're holding hands as we walk along the route Old Hen led us on yesterday, but I feel tongue-tied. So much to tell him, and he won't let me say it. I struggle for another topic. "Tell me about the dance Saturday night."

"Just what you'd expect it to be. All the truly forgettable

songs from our grandparents' era that no one can seem to forget."

"Were they fun to dance to?" I ask.

"Who says I danced?"

"Court did. She said you and Glenna seemed to be having a good time."

Lowell grins. "Jealous?" he asks.

I don't know how to answer that. I shrug.

"Well," Lowell says, "I didn't sulk because you wouldn't come with me, if that's what you mean."

Uh-oh. I feel strange. Dizzy. I stop walking and open my purse, looking for some glucose tablets. Where are they? Did I forget to transfer a new package from my flight bag?

"You're not going to sulk now, are you?" Lowell asks.

With relief I shake my head. The dizzy feeling has passed. But we've come to the place where the road narrows and we leave civilization. I know from our walk yesterday that there aren't any grocery stores between here and the castle ruins. First we have the long walk downhill to reach sea level. Then comes the steeper climb back up again on the promontory.

"I don't think I should go any farther," I tell him. "I— I don't have time."

"What do you mean you don't have time?" Lowell asks. "The bus doesn't leave for two and a half hours."

"You go without me," I say.

He plants his feet apart, crosses his arms, and gives me the old Tough Guy routine. "Look, you wouldn't go to the dance with me. And you let Teresa hang around all day yesterday. Unless she means more to you than I do, you'll go to the castle with me on our last day together."

Why is he making this so hard for me? I look down, unable to speak.

The Tough Guy wilts. He shuffles his feet and clears his throat. "Look, I've written a poem for you, Jane. And I want to give it to you at King Arthur's castle."

A poem? For me?

Hooking his thumbs in the pockets of his jeans, he studies his shoe. "You said you like poetry," he reminds me.

Of course I like poetry! I swallow so my voice won't quiver when I speak. "What kind of poem is it?"

"I guess you'd call it"—he hunches his shoulders by his ears—"a love sonnet."

"Oh, Lowell." I bury my face in his chest, and we hold each other tight. "Give it to me now," I ask his sweater.

"No way. The castle or nothing."

But I feel him slip something in the pocket of my jeans. I think it's the poem, but I don't want to spoil his surprise. If we hurry, I'm sure I'll be all right. With a burst of energy, I race down the hill. When Lowell catches up with me I'm giggling and panting, and I have to hang on to him the rest of the way down the path.

At the bottom I feel awful. Why am I so dizzy? My palms are sweaty, and everything seems blurred. I lean against the flimsy railing and wipe my forehead. Below me I hear breakers lapping against the shore. "I'm hot," I complain.

"It's not much farther now," he says. "See, the ruins are right up there."

"Where?"

"Right up there. Right where you're looking."

"What?"

"The ruins. The ruins of the castle."

I can't think about castles. I'm too hot to think about anything. I've got to get this sweater off.

"Here, let me help you with those buttons," Lowell says. Lowell? What am I doing here with Lowell? I panic, unable to remember. I've got to get away from him and try to think.

"Stop wiggling," he says. "I'll unfasten them for you."

I feel someone pulling at the front of my sweater, and

it makes me angry. *"Leave me alone!"* I scream. *"Don't touch me!"*

I push to get free, but he blocks my path so I have to go the other way. Up. Up those steep steps.

"DUMMY!" someone yells from behind. A familiar voice. Scott, is it? *"DON'T LET HER GO UP THOSE STEPS ALONE! SHE'LL FALL!"*

Footsteps are pounding behind me and I'm desperate to escape. I seize the railing with both hands to help pull myself up the steps. But I'm tired. Too tired.

JANE
Monday, August 19, 7:20 a.m.
Castle ruins, Tintagel

62

Someone forces breath mints in my mouth.

"Ooh," I moan. I'm lying on grass, bathed in icy sweat. People are sitting beside me, but I don't know who they are. Every cell in my body hurts so much I can't even open my eyes.

I feel a tissue wiping my forehead. "You'll be okay," Scott says.

"Shouldn't you give her the bananas?" Lowell asks.

"Not yet," Scott says. "Not until she's awake. She might choke."

Oh no! I've been in reaction! With Scott and Lowell watching. I hear myself crying.

"Take it easy," Scott says. "You'll feel better in a minute."

I open my eyes and struggle to sit up. "I'm cold," I sob. "I'm cold."

Scott tucks my sweater around my shoulders. Lowell yanks off his own sweater to pile on me, too. I'm too busy crying to thank them. "You all right now?" Lowell asks. He's really nervous.

His concern only makes me cry harder. I can't talk.

Lowell turns to Scott. "How come you knew what to do?" he asks.

"I have a sister who's diabetic, too. Court and I have talked a lot about it. Gave us something in common right away." Scott peels a banana and hands it to me. "Think you can handle a real English breakfast?" he says with a wink.

I take the banana reluctantly, prefering to die.

As I nibble, Lowell picks a blade of grass and snaps it apart, like those noisemakers little kids use at their birthday parties. "Well, I'm sure glad you just happened along at the right minute. I couldn't have carried her up those steps alone."

"What do you mean just happened along? Court and I both went looking for you. We were worried when Jane didn't show up for breakfast. Court knew she'd taken her insulin shot and should eat right away. We were afraid you'd done something stupid. Like try to kidnap her, more or less."

"Why didn't anyone tell me she has diabetes?"

Scotts shrugs. "She made Court promise not to tell. She's a lot like my sister. Doesn't want anyone to think she's different."

Lowell takes me by the chin and looks at me with those all-seeing eyes of his. I feel my hair pasted to my head with sweat and know I look like the Teenage Werewolf. "You're different, all right," he tells me. "That's what I like about you." He kisses me lightly on the forehead. "Now no more secrets between us. Okay?"

We're in the waiting room of the medical clinic here in London, and I don't know who's most nervous. Lowell, who's sitting on one side of me, holding my hand. Sylvia on the other side, talking faster than a Joan Rivers monologue. Or Old Hen, who's pacing up and down the hall.

Sylvia has just told Lowell and me about her son who died fifteen years ago when he was seven. A hemophiliac. That explains lots of things about Sylvia, I've decided. And Old Hen, too.

"Medical science has made all kinds of strides since little Harry died," she tells us. "They've isolated a chemical that hemophiliacs lack and have been able to prepare it so that the patients can give themselves a shot when they feel an attack coming on. It used to be, you know, that the only treatment was blood transfusions. And those were only given at a hospital after the patient had undergone lots of pain. If little Harry had been born a few years later, I'm sure the doctors could have saved his life."

I nod, not sure how to respond.

"Our doctor says that the treatment for diabetes is getting better all the time, too. He says they'll have a complete cure for it soon. You'll see."

Suddenly the nurse appears and takes me off alone. Waiting in the examining room for the doctor, I reach into my pocket for a tissue and pull out another kind of paper. Even though it's folded into a postage stamp, I recognize the sheet from one of Lowell's notebooks.

The poem. I've been so out of it today—I slept on the bus nearly all the way from Tintagel to London—that I'd

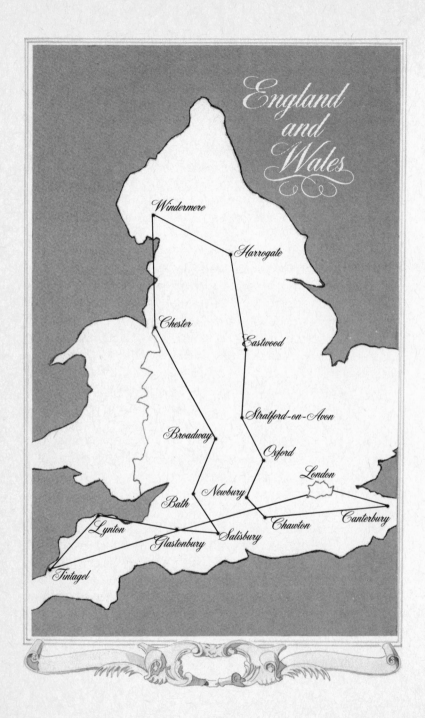

England
and
Wales

Windermere

Harrogate

Chester

Eastwood

Stratford-on-Avon

Broadway

Oxford

London

Newbury

Bath

Chawton

Canterbury

Lynton

Salisbury

Glastonbury

Tintagel

forgotten all about it. My hands shake as I unfold the paper.

I guess I'm smiling when the doctor walks in the room. A short man with broad cheeks and a salt-and-pepper beard. "Well," he says, "your Dr. Phillips was worried about you, but you don't look very sick to me. How do you feel?"

"Wonderful," I say truthfully. I've never felt more wonderful in my life.

JANE
Tuesday, August 20, 4:40 p.m.
O'Hare Airport, Chicago

64

"There's something I have to do," Lowell tells me as we disembark from the 747. "I'll meet you at the baggage claim in a few minutes."

He takes off at a clip, and I wait for Courtney. "Wonder if Buddy will be at the airport in San Francisco to meet me," she muses.

"Listen, Court, I've got to go to the bathroom. They had that 'fasten your seat belt' sign on nearly the whole time. I'm dying."

"Well hurry," she orders. "I'll go pick up our luggage. I'll meet you at the United Airlines counter."

"No, don't do that," I tell her. "I'm supposed to meet Lowell at the baggage claim." But she obviously doesn't hear me. Scott has grabbed her and they've begun an R-rated farewell kiss.

Good old Court. Kissing Scott good-bye in Chicago while she's dreaming of kissing Buddy hello in San Francisco. I figure she'll be tied up for quite a while now. I decide I have plenty of time to do what I have to in the ladies' room before those two are through.

I'm wrong about that, though. Court and Scott have both disappeared when I come out of the bathroom. I hope she won't be too worried about me when I don't show up at the United counter, but Lowell is more important right now. He doesn't have very much time to make his connection to Phoenix, and we still haven't said good-bye.

It's funny how I get disoriented sometimes. I can't remember which direction we came from, and I don't readily see a sign that directs me to the baggage claim. Under normal circumstances, this wouldn't frighten me, but now I'm beginning to panic.

"Jane!" someone calls. It's Teresa, pulling by the hand a woman who is clearly her mother. The older woman is a little bit better-looking and much more stylishly dressed, but they're almost dead ringers for each other. Behind them lurks a man in an expensive-looking three-piece suit who seems to have custody of Teresa's suitcase.

"This is Jane Johnson," Teresa tells her mother.

The woman extends her hand for me to shake. "I'm Darlene Ostermiller. Lucy Beth has told me all about you. I'm so glad the two of you had such a good time together."

I cough up a "How do you do."

"Marty," Mrs. Ostermiller says. "Come meet Lucy Beth's little friend, Jane Johnson. Jane, this is my—our—friend, Marty Black."

Teresa scowls. Marty obviously is no friend of hers.

"How do you do," I say again.

"Well, well, so you're Jane," he says. "How did you like England?"

"Fine," I reply. Your basic generic answer to your basic generic question. I've always felt that questions beginning "How did you like—" should be punished as felonies and sure hope good old Marty learns how to talk to kids before Teresa gets stuck with him as a father. Teresa's picking the nail polish off one of her four remaining sculptured nails. Most of them broke off during her scuffle with Scott.

There's an awkward silence, which Marty feels obliged to fill. "I was just going to take Lucy Beth and her mother out for a welcome-home dinner. How would you like to come along?"

"I'm rushing to catch another plane. Thanks anyway."

Unexpectedly, Teresa bends over and kisses my cheek. "Good-bye, Bernadette. Don't think it hasn't been wonderfully bizarre."

"Good-bye," I reply. "Be sure to look me up when you come west to visit Sin City."

I watch her *clip-clopping* behind her mother and old Marty and feel a terrible pang. What's happened to the way she used to walk? Teresa's spine looks wilted. "I'll write to you," I call.

She turns and gives me a thumbs-up sign with a remaining purple talon.

"Oh, there you are!" Lowell says breathlessly. "I was afraid I'd missed you after I chased all over this airport to get you these." He thrusts a dozen red roses wrapped in green paper at me. One of his famous envelopes is pinned to the outside.

"Oh, Lowell, thank you. No one has ever given me flowers before."

"Thank *you*, Jane. No one has ever saved my life before."

As we kiss, I wonder how I'll ever stand the loneliness. He hasn't even asked for my address. Do summer romances always have to end this way? Maybe Glenna was right. Maybe you shouldn't get involved with people you'll never see again. We pull apart and I whisper in his ear, "I'll miss you."

"Not as much as I'll miss you."

"Good-bye," I say.

"The French say it better," he tells me. "Au revoir."

"Au revoir," I say.

It's not until I've boarded my flight to San Francisco that I have a chance to read his note:

Dear Jane,

Don't think you've heard the last of me. I'm a compulsive letter-writer, remember. I got your address from Scott (who got it from Court), but I'm putting mine on the back of this note in hopes you develop a compulsion, too.

I love you, Lowell

LOWELL
Tuesday, August 20, 6:10 p.m.
Flight to Phoenix

65

Dear Dad,

We have a lot to talk about. Mom. Chris. The baby. And about college next year. I've decided on Stanford, after all. I think I want to be a doctor . . .

Dear Chris,

It's okay about the baby. I've always wanted a little brother or sister . . .

Dear Jane. . . .